CREATION OF DESIRE

Desire, Oklahoma 3

Leah Brooke

MENAGE AMOUR

Siren Publishing, Inc.
www.SirenPublishing.com

A SIREN PUBLISHING BOOK
IMPRINT: Ménage Amour

CREATION OF DESIRE
Copyright © 2009 by Leah Brooke

ISBN-10: 1-60601-461-7
ISBN-13: 978-1-60601-461-5

First Printing: June 2009

Cover design by Jinger Heaston
All cover art and logo copyright © 2009 by Siren Publishing, Inc.

Printed in the U.S.A.

PUBLISHER
Siren Publishing, Inc.
www.SirenPublishing.com

DEDICATION

To my mom for putting up with me and for always being there.

CREATION OF DESIRE

Desire, Oklahoma 3

LEAH BROOKE
Copyright © 2009

Chapter 1

Boone Jackson accepted the slice of cake, smiling at Gracie's broad grin. "It's nice having the girls home again, isn't it?" He had to raise his voice to be heard over the din. Everyone had turned out for the welcome home party Garrett, Drew, Finn and Gracie had thrown for their daughters Hope and Charity.

Gracie handed Boone's brother, Chase, a slice of the cake. "It's wonderful to have them back. Of course their fathers are over the moon to have them home."

Boone took a bite of his cake as Chase laughed. "Yeah, their fathers haven't been more than a few feet from them all night."

Boone looked over to see Hope talking to Jesse Erickson and her sister, Nat Langley, while Garrett looked on, his arm draped around his daughter's shoulder.

Across the room Charity huddled with a beaming Kelly Royal, just back from her honeymoon. Finn had gone to fetch drinks and had delivered them, giving Charity a hug before moving away.

Both Hope and Charity had their mother's petite build but where Gracie was blonde and blue eyed, the girls had their father's coloring. More olive skinned, they had the same brown eyes. Both girls had the cutest dimples and had always been the apples of their daddy's eyes.

"Hope finished her classes last year, but she stayed while Charity finished hers," Gracie told them proudly. "Now they're both home and they say they're staying."

"That's wonderful, Gracie. I know Clay, Rio, and Jesse love having the boys here." Boone gestured toward where the boys, young men actually, sat together laughing and flirting with the girls that kept passing by them. Jesse's nephew, Joe, sat with them.

Boone looked over to where Clay Erickson and his brother, Rio, stood talking to Blade Royal. All three men looked happy, more settled and content than he'd ever seen them.

Gracie laughed. "Yeah, those boys are a handful, and Clay, Rio and Jesse love every minute of it." She sighed. "Isn't it great to see them all so happy?"

"Yeah, it's good to see Clay and Rio have finally found the woman they've waited for." He saw Clay look over at Jesse, the love in his eyes visible even at this distance. Jesse stared back at her husband, her face flushed, the heat in her eyes unmistakable. Feeling like an interloper, he turned back, surprised to find Gracie watching him intently.

She put a hand on his arm, her eyes tender. "You know, I think you and Chase could be just as happy. I hate to see both of you alone when there's a sweet girl just waiting for you." She leaned close and lowered her voice. "I've heard a lot of talk. You'd better get over whatever is keeping you from going after that girl before somebody snatches her out from under your noses."

When she walked away, Boone turned at Chase. "What does she mean by that? Who the hell's after Rachel?"

Although Chase faced him, he didn't meet his eyes. Instead he stared over Boone's shoulder to the table where Boone knew Rachel sat.

"Son of a bitch," he heard Chase say through clenched teeth.

Boone had purposely kept his back to Rachel since entering the diner. After a brief nod in her direction, they'd greeted their friends and moved straight to the counter. He couldn't look at her full lips without wanting to take them with his own or imagining them wrapped around his cock. He couldn't look at her waist length curls without picturing her naked with nothing but those silky curls covering her breasts. His hand itched to hold her curved ass in his hands as he pounded into her. He knew how gorgeous that ass would look when he spread those cheeks and worked his cock into her tight hole. He wanted to see those mocking blue eyes darken with passion as he and Chase gave her more pleasure than she could ever imagine.

He and Chase would hold her afterward, caressing her until she calmed. They would tuck her between them and cuddle next to her warm softness. They would fall asleep to the sound of her breathing next to them.

It would never happen.

Damn it.

Knowing he had no choice but to look, he turned away from Chase's scowl to where Rachel sat talking to Isabel Preston.

Only Isabel no longer sat with her. Two of his friends sat with her now. He glared at Lawton Tyler and his brother, Zach, not liking the way they'd moved their chairs too close to Rachel or the way they eyed her as she spoke to them.

Law leaned toward her, his face way too close to hers as they talked. Boone's jaw clenched at the smile on his friend's face as he played with Rachel's fingers.

"Do you see that?" Chase bit out. "What the fuck are they doing?"

"They're pissing me off. That's what they're doing," Boone told his brother without turning. How could she let them touch her like that? Memories of Mona reached up to choke him, and he ruthlessly pushed them back.

He turned away from the sight of Rachel and his two friends, surprised to see his hand clenched in a fist around the fork. He unclenched it, dropping the fork and shoving the plate away. He didn't want any damned cake.

Scrubbing his hands over his face, he looked over to find Chase still watching Rachel. "She's not for us," Boone said softly. "We can't give her what she deserves."

Chase turned to him then, and Boone winced at the rage and pain on his brother's face. "Law better get his hands off of her."

Lost in thoughts of the woman behind him and what might have been, Boone started when a hand landed heavily on his shoulder. Hunter Ross lowered himself to the stool beside him. "If you don't claim that filly soon, somebody else is gonna saddle her."

Boone glared at him, aware that Chase shifted beside him. It pissed him off even more when Hunter didn't even flinch.

Boone turned away. "I don't want to talk about it."

Out of the corner of his eye he saw Hunter shrug. "That pretty little thing has been chasing you two ever since she came to Desire. If you don't want her, there are plenty of men in this town that would love to get to know Rachel better." He gestured toward the table where Rachel sat, laughing at something Zach said to her.

Boone clenched his teeth so hard his jaw hurt when he saw Hunter eye Rachel. "You included?"

Hunter shook his head and looked down to stare into his coffee. "No. Rachel is the kind of woman a man makes a home with. Rem and I aren't looking for permanent." He chuckled humorlessly. "No woman deserves that."

Before Boone could reply, Hunter got up and moved away. He knew why Hunter and his brother Remington steered clear of relationships.

Their father had been a Dom, an alcoholic and abusive one. While they'd been still in their teens, the men of Desire had run Tom Ross out of town. Their mother, Mary, and her sons had stayed for a while under the protection of the men here but within six months Tom had talked her into going back with him.

Two days after she and the boys had joined him, he'd killed her.

With their father in jail for murder, Hunter and Remington came back to their father's ranch, burying their mother in the town cemetery. Too afraid of being like their father, they never drank. They also never fucked a woman outside Blade's Club, where others could watch, not trusting themselves to be alone with her.

"He's right." Chase sighed and glared again over Boone's shoulder. "Christ, they're hanging all over her. Boone, how the hell are we going to be able to live in this town, seeing her every day with somebody else?"

Boone sighed. He didn't have an answer. He wanted to kill anyone who touched her.

They sat in silence for several minutes, the din of conversations taking place all around them but Boone heard only the sounds coming from the table located about twelve feet behind him.

Rachel's laughter sent a spike of need straight to his groin. His hands tightened into fists when he pictured how the three of them had looked all huddled together. He couldn't really blame them for wanting her. That pissed him off even more. Rachel was a beautiful woman, and no one had stepped forward to claim her.

"Boone. Chase."

Boone twisted on his stool and looked up at Ace Tyler, the town sheriff. "Your brothers better keep their hands to themselves. Rachel doesn't want their attention."

Ace nodded toward Rachel and shrugged. "That's up to her. She's been chasing you two for months so nobody's made a move on her. But it's been almost two years. If you haven't claimed her by now, folks assume you're not going to." He leaned on the counter and nodded toward the table. "Law and Zach know they aren't the only ones interested so they have to move fast."

Boone whipped his head around at that, not liking the smile on Ace's face.

"Time's run out. Either claim Rachel or step back." Ace moved away, and Boone bit back a curse as Chase touched his arm.

"He's right, Boone." Chase leaned close and lowered his voice. "Maybe if we talk to Rachel. Tell her how we feel about her but marriage isn't for us. She might understand."

Boone glared at his brother. "Rachel's no easy lay."

"Did I say she was? I love her just as much as you do. Oh hell."

"What?" Boone spun around as Chase came to his feet. Lawton played with Rachel's curls. Zach had an arm around her shoulders. Both had leaned closer and moved in as if to nuzzle her neck.

"Like hell!" Boone growled and got to his feet.

* * * *

Sitting with Isabel, Rachel watched Boone and Chase walk into the diner. She burned just looking at them. With their broad shoulders and narrow hips, tight buns and muscular thighs, they couldn't help but attract drooling women. Including her. They worked with their hands, and she knew how big and strong those callused hands looked. Every time she saw them she couldn't help but imagine them on her.

When they walked in, their eyes zeroed in on her before turning away. But that quick glance had been enough to have her pulse quicken and her nipples come to attention.

"They are rugged looking, aren't they?" Isabel asked in amusement.

Rachel shrugged and sipped her iced tea. "They're not interested in me."

Isabel smiled. "I almost got burned by the look in their eyes when they saw you."

"Heated looks aren't enough anymore." Rachel blew out a breath. "If they wanted me, Isabel, they would have done something about it by now." She watched as they moved around the room. "I just have to forget about them. I'm not what they want, and I'm tired of wearing my heart out on them."

"We think enough time has been wasted."

Rachel whipped her head around, narrowing her eyes at the look on the older woman's face. "We?"

Isabel smiled mischievously. "Yes, we. A lot of us care very much for all three of you. We've decided to give your men a little push. They're both too stuck in the past to see what's right in front of them."

Rachel stomach fluttered nervously. "Isabel, what are you talking about?" She leaned across the table, careful to keep her voice low as she slid a glance at Boone and Chase. "I don't want anyone to do anything. If Chase and Boone don't want me, fine. I don't want anyone playing games with them or trying to trick them into anything. They've had enough time to make up their minds. Apparently they have and it's not me."

Rachel jumped in her seat when Lawton whispered in her ear. "My friends are hard-headed and stupid."

He grabbed an empty chair and moved it close to her and slid his tall frame into it.

Rachel wished she could be attracted to him. God knows he and his brother looked like models. Both had enough charm to talk a woman into anything. She knew several women came into her lingerie store to buy things to entice Law and his brother, Zach. Their dark good looks combined with the charm they both possessed by the boatload had women falling all over themselves to get close to them. Add the fact that they, along with their brother Ace, owned an oil company and the women came in swarms.

So far they'd been immune.

"Enjoy yourselves, darlings."

Rachel looked up to see Zach helping Isabel from her chair, lifting her hand to his lips. "You look beautiful, as always."

She fluttered her lashes at him. "Flatterer. If I didn't have three jealous husbands—"

"We would have already claimed you for our own," Zach told her easily, flashing a grin.

Rachel watched in amusement as Isabel laughed, "Oh darling, you and that brother of yours would be crying for mercy within a week." She walked away, waving her fingers at them.

"Of that I have no doubt," Zach said to her back, making her laugh again.

Rachel watched Zach nervously as he sat in Isabel's vacant seat.

"What's going on?" Rachel hissed at them, glancing anxiously to where Boone and Chase sat at the counter. She couldn't help but look at their broad shoulders and imagine her hands gripping them in passion as they took her. She started shaking just thinking about it and forced her gaze away.

Law leaned close and reached out to play with her fingers, gripping them firmly when she would have pulled away. Rachel looked down to where their fingers entwined. She wished she felt the kind of electricity that tingled her senses the way Boone and Chase's touch did.

"I wish—," she began.

Law ran his thumb over her hand. "Yeah, honey, so do I."

She glanced at the counter to see that Hunter had joined Boone and Chase. Boone glared at his friend before turning away. Boone glared at everybody lately, especially her.

Looking down to where Law's hand covered hers, she whispered, "I think I know what you're trying to do, but it's useless. Listen. I really appreciate this. Really. But Boone and Chase have already made their decision. It was nice of you to come over here, though." She patted his hand and gestured across the room. "You two better get back over there. The way those women are shooting daggers at me, I won't last much longer."

Zach scooted closer. "Daggers? Boone and Chase have been shooting laser beams at us. The way your men are glaring at us, we may just disintegrate."

Rachel couldn't prevent the bubble of laughter from escaping at Zach's pained expression. She looked toward the counter again to see

Boone and Chase deep in conversation with Ace. Sobering, she sighed. "You two are sweet to care about your friends like this, but trust me. They don't want to get involved with me. Just because I feel something for them doesn't mean that they're going to automatically care about me. I'm fine, really."

Zach leaned closer and rested an arm on the back of her chair. "First, we care about all three of you. Second, don't believe that they don't care for you. They've got some baggage they need to unload. They're both crazy for you but scared to do anything about it."

Law leaned close and ran a finger down her arm. "We're just making them see that they have to make a choice. You or their fear. Let's see which one they choose."

"Uh oh," she heard Zach whisper in her ear. "And the winner is…"

Startled, she looked up in time to see a fierce looking Boone striding toward her, his face set in grim determination. Chase had the same intent look as he strode right behind his brother glaring at Law and Zach, while Boone kept his eyes locked on hers. Rachel sat stunned as they approached, absently aware that Law moved aside. Without a word to anyone, Boone dragged her out of her chair and bent, lowering his shoulder to her stomach. He lifted her over it as he straightened, and strode out of the diner with Chase hot on his heels and Rachel flung upside down over his shoulder.

Chapter 2

What the hell just happened?

One minute she'd been sitting at the table with Lawton and Zach and the next, Boone had yanked her out of the chair and carried her out of the diner.

Surprise kept her frozen and speechless for several minutes before realization set in. Then she started fighting. "What the hell do you think you're doing?" she screeched and began to struggle.

A sharp slap on her bottom had her freezing in outrage. How dare he? "Ow. Are you crazy? What's wrong with you? I wasn't ready to leave. What's with the caveman routine?"

It was hard to sound stern while balancing upside down over a man's shoulder, but Rachel did her best. She also had a good view of his buns from this position and took the time to enjoy it. She's watched those tight buns walk away from her many times, but never had she been this close before. Her fingers itched to grab onto them.

"If you think we'd just sit there and watch you let Law and Zach paw you, you're crazy," Chase growled from behind her.

"What do you care?" Rachel demanded, turning to look up at him. It made her too dizzy so she settled for pounding her fists into Boone's back. "You don't want me. And they didn't paw me. If you don't want to see anyone else touch me, you could have left. Take me back!" She began to struggle again. Her punches didn't seem to be having any impact. She might as well have been punching a wall.

Her bottom stung when Boone slapped it again.

"Be still. When we get back to your apartment, you're going to see just how much we don't want you."

Rachel froze. Did he really mean that? Had Zach been right? Did they really care for her or had they carried her out of the party just because they'd been jealous?

Idiots. She'd been in love with both of them for months. Neither one of them had ever made a move toward her before. Though they both watched her constantly, they'd always kept their distance. She'd finally come to the conclusion that they didn't want her. Now this. If this caveman act had been brought on by only jealousy, she wanted no part of it. She wanted them to come to her because they truly wanted to be with her not because of pressure from others.

"Put me down, damn it." Rachel struggled again, and once again got a smack on her bottom for her efforts. "Stop hitting me!"

Boone's hands tightened on her thighs. "I'm not hitting you. I'm spanking your bottom. Be still."

His hands on her thighs had all sorts of lascivious thoughts going through her mind. He held her firmly, his hands hot through her dress. She had images of his large callused hands running under the material and over her bare thighs.

"What were you thinking, letting Law and Zach paw you like that?" Chase yelled at her.

"It's none of your fucking business, and I already told you they weren't pawing me. Just because you don't want me, ow, stop slapping my ass!"

The heat started to spread and did strange things to her. Her panties became even wetter. The first time they touched her and she'd already gotten aroused. Hell, their touch could hardly be construed as intimate but her body had come alive as though it knew what those hands could do.

"Watch your mouth." Boone growled. "I don't want to hear that kind of language from you."

"Fuck you," Rachel told him succinctly and got another smack on her ass for her effort.

"I warned you," Boone growled.

"You don't want me but you don't want anyone else to touch me. Well, I don't want either of you anymore. I want a man who wants me back. I don't want either one of you, damn it."

"Bullshit," Chase roared. "And if you think we're going to stand by and let somebody else touch you, you'd better think again."

Rachel bobbed on Boone's shoulder as he went up the stairs to her apartment. "Put me down!"

"Chase, get her key out of her purse."

Rachel lifted herself and twisted to see Chase rummaging through her purse for her keys. He must have grabbed it when Boone grabbed her.

Once inside the apartment, Boone went straight to the bedroom and tossed her unceremoniously onto her bed. Coming to her knees, Rachel brushed the hair out of her eyes and glared at them. Her eyes widened when she saw they'd both started undressing.

She'd left a low light burning on her nightstand, the soft glow adding to the unreal atmosphere. The small lamp bathed her bedroom with a delicate luminescence that made everything appear soft and muted except for the two men standing next to her bed. They looked so out of place here and yet so right. Their hard bodies and fierce glittering eyes looked even more harsh and unyielding in the soft light. They looked even more masculine and virile as they began to undress.

Her pulse leapt at the dominant image they portrayed. They looked as fierce as warriors. Both looked at her as though wanting to conquer her. She tried and failed to control her body's response to them but she'd wanted them too long to have any kind of defense against them. She wanted to erase the image of every other woman from their minds and wanted them to want her, to take her, as they've never wanted or taken another. It looked as though she may get her wish. But would it be enough? She didn't want just their bodies. She wanted all of them. Boone and Chase were the epitome of every fantasy she'd ever had rolled into one.

"You say you don't want us anymore. Then why are your nipples hard? Why are you breathing so heavily?" Boone asked mockingly.

"Because I'm mad!" Rachel returned hotly. "You both pissed me off, dragging me out of the party just because other men talked to me." Oh God. They looked so hot and sexy. Moisture flooded her panties and she knew she couldn't hold out much longer.

"I'll bet you're already wet for us, aren't you, sugar?" Chase leered. "When I get my mouth on that pussy, I'm going to lap you up."

"Stop it. I'm tired of your games." Rachel's heart raced. Their wicked smiles made her throb. She had to be the voice of reason. She could do this. This had begun to get way out of control. She held out a hand as if to hold them off. "We need to talk."

Her mouth watered when she got a good look at them. Years of construction work had sculpted their bodies into works of art.

"I don't play games, Rachel," Boone said as he edged closer to her.

Rachel forced herself to speak calmly. "Look, just get dressed and leave. We'll talk tomorrow. You only want me because somebody else does. You'll regret this in the morning."

"More than likely," Boone admitted. "But we're not letting anybody else fuck you."

The control on her temper snapped. "I'll fuck anybody I want to," Rachel shouted. "And there's not a damn thing you can do about it!" She realized immediately that it had been the equivalent of waving a red flag in front of a bull. The look on their faces became hard and determined, their intent to have her unmistakable.

They stripped out of their jeans and boxers and moved toward her. Chase knelt on the bed, and she scrambled off of the other side as he began to crawl toward her, stalking her like a hungry cougar. Brown and sleek, his muscles bunched tightly as though ready to pounce. He paused at the center of her bed, sitting back on his heels, and cutting off that means of escape. She watched, fascinated as he fisted his cock in his hand and began stroking, his eyes never leaving hers. She gulped as she took in his size. His long, thick length looked dark and angry, throbbing its rage. A drop of pre come appeared at the tip, and she licked her lips.

"That's it," he growled deep in his throat. "Get those lips nice and wet so I can fuck that mouth."

Rachel shook as lust gripped her by the throat. She saw a movement out of the corner of her eye. Boone moved around the foot of the bed, edging closer. She couldn't help looking at his even larger cock pointed toward his stomach as he stood with his hands on his hips staring at her. When she saw the glistening tip she grew hotter at how aroused they'd both already become.

Boone edged even closer, cutting off her only other means of escape.

What had their jealousy unleashed?

Boone and Chase looked starved for her, hunters closing in on their prey. Her nipples poked painfully at her lace bra, moisture literally dripping from her as she stared at them. She wanted them more than she'd ever wanted anything in her life. But if they regretted it afterward, it just might kill her.

"You don't really want me."

Boone struck like a cobra, his arm snaring her waist. He tossed her onto the bed, grabbing her wrists in one of his large hands and pulling them over her head. His weight covered her, pinning her to the bed. He lifted her chin until she faced him. His weight felt so good on hers, the hard plains of his body pressing into her softer curves in a way that had her trembling with need. God, he felt so good, better than she'd imagined. She loved his weight on her like this. Suddenly she felt primitive, a woman making demands on her men, needing them to fulfill them.

She spread her legs, automatically arching her hips to feel him cradled against her. She tried to rub her breasts against his chest but couldn't move enough to get the friction she needed. Her breathing became harsh, a combination of excitement and the crushing weight of his body. He levered his weight slightly off of her, allowing her to breathe but not enough to give her room to move.

Next to her, Chase leaned close, brushing her hair back from her face, his eyes even fiercer than before. He held her gaze, and his hands traveled up her arms until he got to her wrists.

"I've got her," he told Boone in a voice she'd never heard from him before. It sent a fresh jolt of need through her.

Boone transferred her wrists to his brother's grip, leaving his hands free. He lifted her hips, pressing his cock against her mound and she gasped.

"Do you feel how much I don't want you?"

His eyes flared so hot they burned her but she couldn't look away. "I've wanted you since the day I met you," he told her through clenched teeth. She swore she could actually see his control slip away. "I look at you and want to fuck you so badly, my legs shake. I wake up in the middle of the night dreaming about your ass and I come all over myself like a teenager. I watch you smile and get hard as a rock picturing your lips wrapped around my cock as I fuck your mouth clear to your throat. Don't you fucking tell me that I don't want you. I want you so badly I can hardly stand it!"

Rachel looked up at him, stunned. A moan slipped out at the images he'd painted in her head. She arched toward him, wrapping her legs around his hips.

He sat back, adjusting until he straddled her. She couldn't look away from the raw lust on his face as he looked down at her. She couldn't breathe, but didn't need to anymore. She only needed them. She'd always known it would be intense with them but she'd badly underestimated just how intense the need would be.

"Yes or no, Rachel?"

Even now they gave her a choice, as if she had one. They could still walk away but she already belonged to them. She had for months. She knew only Boone and Chase could make her feel this way.

She gripped Chase's hands, feeling his own grip tighten and helplessly arched. Her blood boiled, lust for these men bubbling through her. Suddenly she couldn't stand it any longer. No matter what happened, she'd have tonight. One word from her and the men she loved and craved would quench the raging inferno they'd sparked inside her.

"Yes. Damn you. Take me!"

The words had barely left her mouth before Boone ripped her dress in half, exposing her to their gazes.

"God. I could eat her alive." she heard Chase growl from above her. He let go of her hands and moved to her side, reaching for her breasts. Her bra ripped and she felt his hot hands on her.

Boone lifted her, and she gripped his shoulders tightly. They ripped her dress completely off of her, tossing it and her torn bra aside. When they lowered her back to the bed, Chase took her mouth with his, growling, eating at her hungrily as Boone ripped off her panties.

She gripped Chase's wide shoulder to anchor herself as she began to spin out of control. His muscles bunched and shifted as he cupped her breasts, his touch and kiss stealing her breath.

"Sweet heaven," she heard Boone groan as he parted her thighs, wedging his shoulders between them.

Chase lifted his mouth from hers and looked down at her breasts. "You're beautiful, honey. I gotta have a taste." He lowered his mouth to her breasts as Boone parted her folds. She felt their warm breath on her body a second before they touched her. She whimpered in need. She'd been needy too long, starved for them. Every touch felt like more than she could bear and yet not enough.

"Oh God. I can't stand it. It's too much."

Boone devoured her, and she cried out as he licked her from anus to clit. She'd never been touched like this before. She caught her breath, holding onto Chase tightly as she shook, tortured wails coming from deep in her throat. When Boone's tongue stabbed into her she shook even harder, thrashing her head and digging her heels into his back.

Chase nipped at her breasts, using his tongue to soothe the slight stings. He used his mouth on her everywhere except where she needed it most, covering her breasts with little stings until her nipples became so tight and needy they ached.

"Please," she begged, gripping his head as she arched toward his mouth.

Her hips lifted of their own violation as Boone pressed a thick finger into her dripping opening. He stroked the quivering muscles inside. She tried to rock her hips but he held her immobile while he fucked her with his finger, swiping her folds with his tongue the entire time.

She'd never felt like this before, hadn't known it would be possible to get so lost in passion. It felt like a thousand little sparks sizzled through her body. She shook with such force it almost scared her. She barely recognized the sounds coming from her throat as her own as she cried out and demanded, whimpered and begged.

When Chase closed his teeth over a nipple, she jolted. Boone sucked her clit into his mouth and she bowed, screaming as huge waves of almost unbearable pleasure passed through her. She cried out her ecstasy, moaning as they prolonged it. She whimpered as it passed, her body still quivering from the magnitude of her climax. Almost immediately they aggressively began to build her arousal again. Still not recovered from the first, she became a creature of need and whimpered helplessly.

That just spurred them on.

Chase's mouth and hands became even more demanding. When he nibbled at her neck, she arched it to give him better access. She pushed her breasts higher into his hands, already moving toward her next release.

Boone had her thighs spread wide, his mouth greedy as he consumed her, carefully avoiding her clit and using his fingers to stroke inside her. She could feel herself clenching on them but couldn't seem to stop. She no longer controlled her own body. They did, playing her and drawing out responses she'd never known and wouldn't have believed herself capable of.

Boone seemed determined to draw every bit of moisture from her, and she could do nothing but give him whatever he wanted. Her groans and whimpers filled the room, her breathing ragged as she struggled to fill her lungs.

When his mouth left her, she cried out in distress only to feel him start to press his length into her. It had been a long time for her and her body struggled to accept him.

"Easy, sugar. You can take me," Boone told her tenderly, his voice tight with tension. "Christ, you're so tight."

Chase's mouth lifted mere inches from hers, and he placed a hand over her stomach. "Relax. Let Boone in, baby. We'll take good care of you." His hand moved over her stomach and beyond. When he used a callused finger to tease her clit, she began thrashing.

"I can't. I can't," she cried hoarsely.

"Sure, you can, baby. Let us love you." Chase closed his lips around a nipple.

Boone stroked deeper and deeper, stretching her more with each thrust until he had his length pressed fully into her. She felt the tingling sparks begin again. "Oh God!" She thrashed on the bed, fisting her hands in the bedding as she fought to anchor herself. Then she flew.

Her muscles clenched on Boone, and she heard his hoarse cry as he came. He kept stroking while Chase continued to torment her breasts, sucking and pinching at her too sensitive nipples. Boone held himself deep inside her, and she couldn't stop rocking her hips on him.

She couldn't take much more. She couldn't stop.

Her body trembled uncontrollably but they kept making her want more. She couldn't stand any more. She couldn't live without it.

Boone withdrew from her and flipped her to her stomach. Chase moved in to take Boone's place between her legs and pulled her bottom high and thrust into her from behind. She cried out at the pleasure and buried her face into a pillow, her hands curled tightly on the slats of the headboard.

Oh God, she felt so full. She found herself meeting his thrusts as he slammed into her over and over.

Boone reached under her and stroked a nipple, pinching lightly.

"Oh God," she whimpered.

Chase thrust into her to the hilt and held her hips steady. "Tell us you want us," he growled. "Tell us you don't want anyone else to have you like this."

"Move," Rachel demanded and tried to thrust her hips, but they were held immobile.

"Say it," Boone roared.

"I want you," she sobbed. "Please."

"Only us?" he demanded.

"Only you. Please."

"And no one else can have you?" Chase demanded hoarsely.

"No, just you!" Rachel screamed desperately, then sobbed, "Please." Why didn't he just shut up and move?

Rachel cried out when Chase started to thrust again, but froze when a finger pressed at her puckered opening.

"No, don't." She tried to pull away, but Chase held her firmly. She'd never had anything in her ass before, and the thought of these two touching her there would be more than she could handle.

The deep stroking stopped.

"We're both going to take your ass, baby. I need to loosen you up," Boone told her, his voice sounding raw and gravelly.

"I've never," Rachel began. Oh God. How could she stand it?

"Good. Now relax so I can stretch you."

A shiver went through her when Boone began to press a thick finger into her bottom. Relax? Her lower body bloomed as Chase's thrusting resumed.

"Oh God. It's too much." They touched her everywhere and she felt herself spiraling out of control. Never had she had her body taken over like this. She felt helpless to do anything but respond. The feeling of her rear being invaded staggered her. She felt primitive and carnal, becoming nothing more than a creature of lust, caring about nothing but the pleasure they continued to force her to accept.

"No, baby. It's not too much. You can take it. Let go." Boone told her as he moved his thick finger inside her.

When he withdrew from her bottom, she whimpered at the loss. She'd never wanted anything to do with anal play before, had never allowed it. Boone made her crave it now. She pushed back, trying to get him to touch her there again. Knowing Chase watched excited her even more.

When two fingers pressed into her, she arched and cried out. "Oh yeah," Boone said tightly. "We've got to stretch this tight ass, baby." He reached under her and pinched a nipple as he pushed his fingers deep.

Chase slowed his strokes. "Do you know how hot it is to watch Boone's fingers disappear into your tight ass?" Chase growled. "I can't wait to get my cock in there. Let Boone open your bottom, sugar. We want all of you."

They drove her wild, turning her into a wanton she didn't recognize. "It hurts," Rachel whimpered even as she pushed back on Boone's fingers. "It feels good and hurts at the same time. More, faster."

Their thrusting in both openings increased to a furious pace. Rachel couldn't believe how her body opened to them so completely. The too full, too forbidden feeling of having them invade both openings had her bucking wildly, her body shaking uncontrollably. Knowing they both watched Chase's cock disappearing into her pussy and Boone's fingers disappear into her bottom made all her inhibitions fly away. When Chase reached under her and pinched her clit, she cried out again, clenching on both men where they invaded her.

Chase roared. He plunged his cock deeply inside her, holding it there and she knew he'd followed. Her arms buckled. Slumping forward on the bed, Rachel struggled to catch her breath, moaning as they both pulled out of her and collapsed on the bed next to her.

Lying between her two lovers, she still trembled. They stroked and caressed her rapidly cooling body, dropping kisses all over her face, neck and shoulders.

When she started to drift off, she heard Chase's teasing voice. "Don't you fall asleep on us. Boone and I aren't done with you yet."

Oh God.

Chase lifted her as though she weighed nothing and carried her to the shower, lowering her feet to the floor and steadying her when she swayed. "You are so beautiful, sugar." Chase nipped her bottom lip, making her smile.

"And you are so sexy." She ran her hands over his chest, marveling at the play of muscles as he soaped her.

She returned the favor. She soaped him all over and rinsed him, reveling in the freedom to touch him this way. Running slick soapy hands over each other soon had them both aroused again.

"I want to taste you," she told him, running a hand down his length, smiling seductively as it jumped in her hand.

The gold in Chase's light brown eyes flared with heat. "Sugar, I would love to feel that hot little mouth on my cock."

Rachel dropped to her knees and took him in her mouth as the warm water washed over them both, loving the groans he made as she stroked her tongue over him. She sucked him as deeply as she could, determined to give back the pleasure they'd given her. She wanted to steal their control as they'd stolen hers.

She felt a blast of cool air as the shower door opened. "If that's not a beautiful sight," Boone murmured hoarsely. "I hope I'm next."

Rachel answered by reaching over to stroke his impressive cock, and was rewarded with a groan.

Chase held her head with both hands, stroking steadily into her mouth. She had to open her mouth wide to take him inside. She sucked gently, using her tongue on the sensitive underside. The hands on her hair tightened, and his groans had her slit weeping once again.

Boone uncurled her hand from his thick shaft with a soft, "let me get cleaned up, baby."

Rachel felt Boone's eyes on her as he showered, watching her as she sucked his brother's cock, and it made her even hotter. It made her feel powerful and desired. Having two men at once added layers to her arousal that she'd never expected. Loving them both and knowing they watched whatever the other did to her or what she did to them added to her already overwhelming lustful urges. She used both her hands and mouth on Chase, determined to drive him crazy and to put on a show for Boone.

"Oh, sugar. Your mouth feels so good on my cock. That's it, Rach, take me deeper."

Chase fucked her mouth harder now and she gripped the base of his cock so he wouldn't push too far.

"Oh, Rach. Fuck. I'm coming."

He erupted and Rachel swallowed frantically. He pulsed against her tongue, and his firm grip on her hair became softly caressing. The shudders that went through him made her feel wanton and powerful and very desired.

"Oh, sugar. That mouth is amazing."

He pulled her to her feet and kissed her hungrily, making her heart pound. She couldn't help but rub her nipples on his chest. When he lifted his head, dimples slashed as he grinned.

"When you and Boone finish showering, I'm gonna eat that pussy. It's my turn." With another quick kiss and a blast of cool air he left. She watched him leave, speechless and trembling with anticipation.

Boone pulled her back against his rock hard chest, his calloused hands coming around to cup her breasts. Rachel leaned back against him, arching her neck as he lowered his head. Those rough hands felt even better than she'd imagined, and she knew she'd never again be able to look at his hands and not get aroused. His mouth hungrily ate at hers, his tongue stroking deep, nibbling at her lips teasingly, only to claim her mouth demandingly again.

He pinched her nipples lightly, making her cry out. His long thick length pressed into her back, and she pressed back against him, moving her body to stroke him, letting her long hair rub over him. When she tried to turn in his arms she found she couldn't budge.

"But I want to suck you."

Boone groaned and loosened his hold as he allowed her to turn and tease his mouth as he'd done to hers. When she drew his tongue into her mouth and sucked gently, his cock jumped against her stomach.

"Christ, Rachel. You're a witch."

She smiled against his mouth and again lowered to her knees. Being able to finally touch them like this went straight to her head like wine. She'd waited too long to have them. Greedy to have it all, she let her hands roam, touching him everywhere. In her thirty years, no one had ever come close to making her feel what Boone and Chase could make her feel with a glance. Having them here with her now, naked and hungry, had her feeling more alive than she'd ever felt, more desired than she'd thought possible. And very, very greedy.

Finally all her dreams were coming true.

Rachel teased Boone mercilessly, using her hands and mouth to elicit first moans as she kissed and licked at his length, then deep groans when she took him into her mouth, closing on him, but not sucking. She could tease, too, and wanted him wild. She smiled when the threats started, her body thrilling as they got more and more erotic.

"Come on, baby. Suck me."

"Please, baby. I want to feel that hot mouth suck me deep."

"Rachel, damn you. Suck me!"

"Suck me, damn it. I swear, baby, when I get you back into the bedroom, I'm fucking your ass so hard you'll never forget."

Too aroused to deny him or herself any longer, she began sucking, her hand curling around his full sack, gently caressing. She used her other hand to stroke the base of his shaft in rhythm with her mouth.

Her clit swelled and throbbed as she pleasured him. When his big thighs trembled, her nipples ached. His harsh groans made her slit weep.

He roared as he exploded, his hands gripping her head as his whole body shook. She loved the way he pulsed against her tongue and thrilled at the deep tortured groans coming from his throat and the way his big body shuddered. She swallowed his erotic taste as she reached down to pluck at her nipples. Already tender from their earlier ministrations, it didn't take much to have the pleasure arrowing to her slit.

Boone lifted her and pulled her hands away from her breasts, and she cried out in protest.

"But I need—"

He drew her out of the shower with him and quickly dried them both. "I know what you need, baby. You're going to pay for teasing me like that," he told her darkly, picking her up and carrying her into the bedroom, his eyes fierce with intent. He sat on the edge of the bed and flipped her effortlessly over his lap, and she cried out, startled. What was he doing?

"My thoughts exactly," Chase murmured as he moved to kneel next to her. "She needs to have a red ass for letting Law and Zach touch her like that."

"Good point," Boone agreed. "I almost forgot about that. She deserves a spanking for teasing me in the shower. I guess it's gonna have to be a little more intense than I'd planned."

"Oh God." Rachel groaned, embarrassed to her toes that the thought of them spanking her turned her on. Just being over Boone's knees this way, knowing she had no defense against whatever they chose to do to her ass, feeling their eyes on it, made her pussy weep. Rachel had frozen in surprise at being put over Boone's lap but now she began struggling, not wanting them to see how wet thcir threat had made her.

"No. You can't do this!"

"Wanna bet?" Boone growled.

"I don't want to be spanked, damn it." Rachel fought and twisted uselessly. She couldn't move an inch. A sharp slap landed on her bottom. "Ouch. Fuck!"

"I've warned you about that mouth," Boone said and landed another slap.

The heat from her bottom spread exquisitely, much to her horror. Oh God, what was wrong with her? Draped over Boone's hard thighs, her bottom on display for both of them shouldn't be turning her on this way. The heat spreading from her spanking only made it worse. Several more slaps in rapid succession had her bottom stinging, the heat incredible.

She found herself lifting her bottom for Boone's punishment and clenching her thighs together as she tried to find relief. Boone pressed a hand down on her bottom cheeks to hold her still when she tried to rub her clit on his thigh. She moaned in frustration and tried desperately to break his grip as his hand held the heat in.

"Are you going to let anyone else touch you?" Boone demanded.

"Let me up."

Another series of slaps landed.

"Wrong answer, sugar," Chase taunted.

"I saw some oil in the bathroom," Boone drawled. "You finish her spanking, while I work on her ass."

A dark hunger and thrilling fear went through Rachel at Boone's words. She found herself transferred to a demonically gleeful Chase who seemed to get devilish enjoyment out of reddening her ass. To her amazement and utter horror, his repeated slaps had her so aroused, she found herself reaching for another orgasm. The hotter her bottom got, the wetter she got until she could literally feel her juices flow from her. Her clit throbbed painfully, and she couldn't prevent herself from seeking Chase's touch, lifting to him over and over. Boone had retrieved the oil and knelt beside her.

"Are you going to let anyone touch you again?" the usually playful Chase growled.

"No, no. Only you and Boone. I promise. I need to come. Please." Rachel sobbed and twisted, frantic to come.

"Spread your legs. Show us how much you enjoyed your spanking."

Rachel had moved past being embarrassed about how much the spanking had turned her on. All she cared about now was relief. She spread her thighs wide and two thick fingers slid into her.

"Oh yes," Chase hissed as he stroked her pussy. "Rachel loves having her ass spanked."

"Spread her," Boone demanded. "Let's see how much she loves having it fucked!"

Rachel froze. Her heart leapt to her throat when Chase withdrew from her and placed a hand over each of her cheeks, making the heat spread even more. She gasped as he spread them, exposing her puckered opening to their gazes.

Rachel had never felt so exposed or so vulnerable in her life. "No," she whimpered when she felt the oil drip down her crease. "I can't do this."

"Yes, you can, baby." Boone's voice managed to be both firm and gentle at the same time. "Remember how you teased me in the shower, how aroused you got when I told you I was going to take your ass?"

"Ohhh," Rachel moaned when he poised a blunt finger at her tight opening. The oil had done its job, and when he pressed, his finger slid all the way inside her.

"Oh my God," Rachel groaned. She grabbed onto Chase's leg, and began to move back and forth on the finger invading her.

"Move," she sobbed.

"Jesus," she heard Chase mutter. "Sugar, you're so hot. Damn, that's beautiful."

"She's got a helluva grip, too," Boone said. "Fuck. I can't wait to get my cock in here."

Both men continued to watch her ass being invaded as Boone added a second, then a third finger, stretching her and adding more oil as he continued to thrust into her.

"You like having your ass stretched, don't you, baby?" Boone asked as he pushed into her.

"Oh God. Yes!"

"Does it burn, baby?"

"Yes. More!"

"You like us having our way with you, don't you, baby? We can have everything, can't we?"

"Yes. Anything. Just let me come."

"Your ass looks so beautiful swallowing my fingers, baby. Are you ready for me to shove my cock in here?"

"Please."

Boone withdrew his fingers from her ass, and she clenched at the emptiness, her trembling increasing by the second.

Chase stood with her, positioning her on her knees on the edge of the bed and pressing her shoulders to the mattress. He held her shoulders firmly as Boone moved in behind her, spreading her legs to his satisfaction before poising his cock at her oiled opening.

"Please don't hurt me," Rachel whimpered even as her bottom pressed back against him.

"Baby, this is going to hurt so good, you're not going to be able to live without it," Boone promised.

Rachel shivered as Boone began to push past the tight ring of muscle, whimpering at the erotic burn.

Chase's hands moved her long hair aside and caressed her back, crooning to her as she trembled beneath his hands. "Relax, sugar. Let Boone inside. We're going to make you feel so good, honey. I promise."

Boone's hands gripped her hips tightly as he rocked his hips, plowing deeper inside her with every deliberate thrust. "You're killing me." His voice was raw with need. "So fucking tight. Christ, she's clamped on me like a vice."

Rachel's whimpers and groans grew louder with each thrust until she lost all semblance of herself. The touch of her lovers and their beloved voices, one harsh and tense, the other tender and soothing became her world.

She needed both to survive this. When her body opened for Boone's invading length, his hoarse triumphant cry and dark erotic words had her pushing back against him. She sobbed as she strove to satisfy her greedy hunger even as she struggled to adapt to the overwhelming burn of being stretched.

Chase's hands and voice anchored her when fear of her unconditional and absolute surrender might have overwhelmed her. Instead her body made its own demands, which spurred Boone even more. His arm felt like a steel band around her waist as he lifted her, handling her as though she weighed nothing as he pulled her back against his chest.

"Oh God. I can't," she sobbed. "I'm going to—"

"Come," Boone growled as he sat on the edge of the bed still embedded inside her.

Sitting on him like this forced his hot steely length even deeper and Rachel came, screaming in ecstasy as she flailed wildly, fearing the strength and completeness of her orgasm.

"No! Make it stop," she begged as it took her over.

"Fuck," Boone growled. "Her ass is so tight and she's milking me too hard. Fuck," he roared again as he spurted, pulsing deep inside her.

Her orgasm lasted forever and yet not long enough.

She felt Chase's mouth on her breasts as she came down and weakly reached for him, tangling her hands in his hair while he sucked and lightly bit her nipples. Unbelievably, her body started to come to life again.

"I can't take anymore," she protested weakly.

Chase rose up to kiss her, his mouth harsh and possessive on hers. "Now I get to take that tight ass while Boone plays with your pussy."

She was flipped back onto her knees before Chase's words registered.

"I can't come anymore," she moaned as Boone withdrew from her ass and Chase took his place.

Rachel watched Boone go into the bathroom as Chase began to press his cock into her recently vacated bottom.

"That's it, sugar. Let me in. Oh, honey, you feel so good." Chase hissed. "Fuck, Rachel. Damn you're tight."

The full feeling of having his cock thrusting into her ass had her crying out. She grabbed the sheets as his thrusts became harder. God, it felt so forbidden, so erotic. She'd never dreamed of doing such a thing before and now knew she could never again live without them taking her this way.

When Boone came back, she found herself being lifted once again. Chase sat on the edge of the bed with her on his lap, his cock pressed firmly into her bottom. It burned so hot she thought she would die of it. He spread his legs and hers, and Boone moved into position between them.

Boone knelt in front of her, his eyes full of dark intention as he spread her folds and ran his fingers over her slit.

"Our baby loves to have her ass fucked. Look at how wet she is."

When he spread her thighs even wider, she moaned. "Oh God, I can't."

"Sure, you can, sugar." Chase's teasing voice became low and tense.

The first touch of Boone's fingers on her slit had her squirming and clenching, wailing her pleasure. She'd never known such pleasure existed.

Boone continued to use his hands on her ruthlessly, making her twist and squirm harder, effectively forcing her to ride Chase's cock. Chase bit off curses as his hands tightened on her. She felt too full, Chase's cock pressed too deep, Boone's fingers too devastating as they pushed inside her, traced her folds, rolled her clit.

She cried out for more.

Chase's hands covered her breasts, and he began to pinch and tug at her nipples, sending a jolt of raw lust through her. Her clit began to throb painfully as she rode Chase even harder.

He cursed steadily now, his groans mixing with hers, both growing louder and more desperate. When Boone took her clit between his thumb and forefinger and pinched her, Rachel froze, her body becoming a shimmering ball of lust. He pinched her clit sharply and she burst, clenching tightly and pulsing as she flew apart in an explosion a shimmering sparks.

She heard Chase's hoarse cry as he filled her with his hot seed, his hands wrapping tightly around her as his cock pulsed in her bottom.

It could have been minutes or hours later when Boone lifted her from Chase's lap. She couldn't prevent a whimper when Chase's cock slid out of her. Boone laid her on the bed, and Chase ran a hand over her soothingly while Boone disappeared into the bathroom. He came back with a washcloth and cleaned her, gently parting her as he washed between her legs. She shuddered and moaned, trying to move away but he held her until he'd finished.

Chase moved away as Boone settled her under the covers with him and gathered her close.

"Come here, baby. I want to hold you."

She was dimly aware of Chase's return from the bathroom. He turned off the lights and settled in on the other side of her. Her body still quivered and they continued to use their warm hands to caress her until little by little the shivers lessened.

Warm and sated and in bed with the men she loved, Rachel smiled into the darkness and sighed.

A heartbeat later she fell sound asleep.

Chapter 3

Rachel woke to the sound of the shower running and the smell of coffee. She smiled, remembering the previous night and opened her eyes, glancing around for her lovers. Seeing neither, but hearing sounds from the kitchen and bathroom, she grinned and jumped out of bed.

She looked at the clock, and grimaced. She had to start getting ready to open the store. No time this morning for sex, but she did have time for a cuddle. With that in mind she reluctantly headed for the kitchen instead of the shower. They'd make up for the missed sex later.

She came to a halt when she saw Boone sitting at her table, frowning into his coffee cup. He'd already dressed, his hair damp, so he'd obviously been up for a while.

"Good morning." She smiled and started toward him, expecting him to pull her onto his lap.

He flicked her a glance and looked back down into his cup. "Good morning, Rachel. We need to talk."

Rachel froze. He wouldn't meet her eyes. Changing direction, she moved to the coffee pot, glancing at him out of the corner of her eye. He hadn't moved. After pouring herself a cup of coffee, she hesitantly joined him at the table.

"Is something wrong?" she asked, a chill of fear running down her spine. Why didn't he smile? Did he regret last night?

He sighed. "No, baby. I just wanted to talk to you about last night."

She didn't care for the way he wouldn't meet her eyes, but continued to stare into his coffee. What had happened to the fierce lover that had taken her so completely last night? Where was the man that had slept holding her tightly against him all night long?

Chase appeared, slipping his shirt on. He moved to the coffee pot, flicking her a wary glance, and mumbling 'good morning' as he passed.

Something had to be very wrong.

"Last night was wonderful," she began carefully. "Wasn't it?" *Please don't tell me you regret it.*

Chase sipped his coffee, leaning against the counter as he regarded her steadily.

Boone finally looked up. "Last night was the best night of my life."

"Mine too," Chase added and looked away.

"I don't understand." Rachel whispered, glancing back and forth between them. They certainly didn't look like they'd both just had the best night of their lives. "You say last night was great but you both look like somebody kicked your puppy and neither one of you has even touched me this morning."

Boone sighed and reached out, touching the sleeve of her robe. "We just want to make sure you understand what happened last night. Chase and I really care about you, Rachel, but we're not looking for a permanent relationship."

Rachel kept her features carefully blank as she felt her insides wither and die. They considered last night a mistake. She could see it in Boone's eyes. She'd considered last night the beginning of something wonderful and they regarded it as a mistake.

"We'd like to keep seeing you, but we just want to make sure you understand that, at least for now, we can't promise anything. It's not that we'll be seeing anyone else, though."

She heard Boone as though from a distance as her heart shattered into a million pieces.

Chase looked up at her, his eyes sad. "We need to explain some things to you. We really care about you and want to see you but we're not ready for anything more just yet."

Boone covered her hand with his. "I hope you understand, baby, and will let us be part of your life."

Silence filled the room for the several long moments it took Rachel to find her voice. When she did, it was laced with fury. "Oh, I understand all right. You want somebody to fuck without actually committing to anything!" She stood and flung her cup at the wall, hearing it shatter as she faced both men. "The only part of my life you want to be a part of is my sex life. Last night was your way of making sure nobody else would have me even though you don't want me for yourself."

She stormed to the doorway and spun to face them again. "After the way you pulled your caveman act and carried me out of the diner, no one in this town will ever be interested in me. That's all you wanted. They'll all consider me your property and won't come near me again. I knew you didn't really want me. I knew it and I still fell for it. I can't believe I'm that stupid! All you wanted to do was put a no trespassing sign around my neck and walk away."

She fought the tears that threatened and clenched her hands into fists. "So you don't want a relationship with me. Fine. I never asked you for one, and I'm not mad that you don't want one. What pisses me off is that after all the time you've known me, you have so little respect for me that you waited until after you spent the night fucking me to tell me that you don't want me for anything else. Not only that, but you only fucked me so no one else would."

"Rachel, please. Let's talk about this. It's not like that at all." Boone stood and step toward her, but she stepped back.

"Don't you fucking touch me," she fumed, shaking with anger and pain. "Get out! I don't want to ever see either one of you ever again." Not gonna happen in a town this size, but she would do her best. Seeing them every day would be unbearable.

"Rachel, sugar," Chase began and moved closer.

"Don't you sugar me, you jerk. I hate you. I hate both of you. You're both liars, and I'm sorry I ever met either one of you. Get out."

"That's enough, damn it!" Boone grabbed the front of her robe and lifted her to her toes. "Everything we said to you last night was the truth. We've never lied to you. We want you, damn it. We're just asking you for a little time."

"Take all the time you want." She sneered and pulled away from him. "Take the rest of your life. I don't give a shit. I've had enough of both of you. I don't want either one of you anymore."

Chase reached out and grabbed her, pulling her tightly against him. She fought not to respond to his body against hers, her breasts crushed against his chest. "Now who's the liar? I can prove you're lying. I can have you begging me to take you again."

Rachel knew he spoke the truth but tried desperately not to show it. She had to make them leave before she did something incredibly stupid. She knew she'd never forgive herself if she gave in to them now. She curled her lip at him. "Don't you mean you'll have me begging you to fuck me?" She shrugged. "Sure, you're good, but so are a lot of other men, and they might actually stick around after they fuck me." She forced her expression to remain cool as she saw temper flare in his eyes.

"Watch yourself, honey."

"Why?" She looked at both of them disdainfully. "All you wanted was a fuck. You got it. So did I. Thanks for a good time. Now get out."

"I ought to put you over my knee for talking like that," Chase told her through clenched teeth.

Rachel laughed humorlessly. "You don't have the right to do that. But I'll pass your suggestion on to the next man I fuck. How's that?" She lowered her voice. "Maybe he'll like having me over his lap so much he'll never want to leave."

Boone clenched his hands into fists, then closed his eyes and took a deep breath before unclenching them. "Rachel, we just need a little time. We're crazy about you."

Rachel cursed herself when she swallowed the lump in her throat and knew she didn't have much time. "Well I no longer care about either of you. Get the fuck out. Now!"

Boone eyed her, and she ruthlessly ignored the pain in his eyes. "Come on, Chase. Let's let her calm down."

Chase muttered curses, his gaze desperate as he passed her but she just glared at him.

"Baby," Boone began, "we'll talk later."

"Yeah, when hell freezes over. *Get out.*"

Rachel managed to keep her features hard and cold until the door closed behind them. Moving painfully, she locked it and crumpled to the floor as the tears she'd kept at bay broke free, and she wept as her heart shattered.

* * * *

Rachel couldn't believe how often she saw Boone and Chase now.

In a town as small and close knit as Desire, she saw practically everyone at some point during the week, but hadn't run into them that often. It made her realize just how hard they'd worked in the past to avoid her.

She had no such luck in avoiding them.

Chase just happened to be in the grocery store when she shopped, something that had happened only a handful of times since she'd moved to town.

"Chase is looking at you like he'd like to eat you up," Isabel murmured as she rang up her order.

Rachel looked over to where Chase stood staring at her, angry at herself because she'd known right where he'd been standing. "He had a bite and spit it out. How much do I owe you?"

When she went to the bank to make the deposit for her store, Boone came in and stood in line right behind her.

"Baby, can we come over tonight to talk to you?" he asked next to her ear.

Rachel turned and walked out of the bank without a word.

She couldn't eat at the diner without running into them. She went to the Erickson's one night to talk to Jesse and they both showed up to help Clay, Rio and the boys with something next door. If she didn't know better, she'd swear the whole town conspired against her as she ran into Boone and Chase every day.

Her anger had worn off and depression set in, and she became more and more lethargic. By the time she closed the store every day, she found herself struggling to keep her eyes open.

One day, about six weeks after their night together, Boone and Chase walked into her store just before closing.

"I'm getting ready to close. If you're shopping for your current lay, you're going to have to hurry. I'm tired and I want to go home."

She turned away but Boone grabbed her arm and spun her back around to face him. His angry scowl blurred, and she watched as though from a distance as his angry scowl became concern, then everything went black.

She opened her eyes to find herself lying on the carpet with Boone and Chase leaning over her. She fought not to react to the concern on their faces and struggled to get up.

"Stay still, baby." Boone touched her cheek softly. "What happened? Are you sick?"

"We'd better get her to Doc Hansen's." Chase moved as though to lift her.

"I'm fine." Rachel fought against their hands as they tried to restrain her and stood, moving away from them. "I got busy and forgot to eat. That's all."

They looked at each other, and then back at her.

Boone's face tightened. "I still think you should let Dr. Hansen take a look at you. You're white as a sheet, and you look like you've lost weight."

Rachel turned her back to them and frantically flipped through her mental calendar. Oh God. She couldn't be. She carefully schooled her features before turning back to them. "I already talked to Dr. Hansen," she lied. "I'm anemic. He gave me some vitamins. I just forgot to eat. Was there something you wanted? If not, I'd like to close up."

"Honey, when are you going to talk to us?" Chase asked softly. "We've tried to talk to you so many times but you never want to listen."

"How about if we take you to the hotel for dinner?" Boone asked. "We can talk there."

Rachel sighed tiredly. She wanted to get away from them before they suspected the truth. Now she *would* have to go see the doctor. "I'm tired. I don't feel like going out. I don't feel like having company or talking. I want to grab something to eat, take a bubble bath and go to bed."

She couldn't prevent the shiver of awareness that went through her when Chase touched her arm.

"Honey, please. Boone and I care about you very much. We've given you more than enough time."

"We really need to talk, Rachel." Boone sighed impatiently. "You've avoided us long enough."

"We have nothing to talk about. You wanted an easy fuck, and you got one."

"Damn it, Rachel," Boone growled. "That's not what happened between us that night, and you damned well know it. We care about you. Give us a chance to work this out. Give us a chance to be together."

Rachel fought the urge to give in. She wanted to laugh at the irony. If she hadn't been feeling the effects from what she suspected happened that night, she just may have given in to them. Now she just wanted to sleep.

"You care so much about me that you left skid marks on my floor on your way out the door." She sighed. "Look, I'm tired. I just want to go to bed."

She began to close up the store, glad that they helped. She felt dead on her feet by the time they'd finished. Boone and Chase followed her up to her apartment as she dragged herself up the stairs. When they got to the top, Boone nuzzled her lips with his. "This isn't over, baby, but I can see you're too tired tonight to talk about it. We will talk, though. Make no mistake, this isn't over. Get some sleep. We'll see you tomorrow."

Chase moved in and she felt his lips on her forehead. "Go to bed, honey. When you're rested, we'll talk."

* * * *

Rachel sat in the back room of Indulgences with Jesse and Kelly, reaching for another tissue as the tears continued to fall.

"Thanks again for letting me borrow Brittany today. I've already placed an ad for someone full time." She laughed humorlessly. "I guess I'm really going to need it now."

"Oh, honey. Everything is going to be fine. We're all here for you." Jesse wrapped her arm around Rachel's shoulders as she handed her a glass of juice.

"Thanks. Can you believe it? I'm pregnant." Rachel smiled through her tears. "I'm going to have a baby."

Kelly smiled, tears in her own eyes as she covered Rachel's hand with her own. "I'm so happy for you, Rachel. You're going to be a wonderful mommy."

"A mommy." Rachel sighed, and then scowled. "How am I going to keep it from Boone and Chase?"

"You can't." Jesse said softly. "That wouldn't be fair to them. It's only a matter of time before they see the evidence for themselves anyway. Have they still been trying to get you to talk to them?"

"Yes," Rachel admitted. "But I don't want to talk to them. They don't want a relationship with me, and loving them the way I do, I can't just pretend I don't want more. Besides, now I've got someone else to think about." She pressed a hand to her still flat stomach.

They'd all been there the night six weeks ago when Boone and Chase had stormed out of the diner with her. As she'd predicted, after that everyone had considered her off limits. Not that she minded. She had no interest in anyone but them, but had finally admitted to herself that it was futile.

"They both know that I'm not interested in having them in my life as just sex partners."

"Here you go." Nat rushed into the back carrying a bag from the drugstore. "Prenatal vitamins and a box of saltines." She smiled at Rachel. "Staples for every pregnant woman."

"Thanks for picking them up, Nat. I really appreciate it."

"Now there's going to be rumors all over town that I'm pregnant because I picked up prenatal vitamins at the drugstore." She laughed. "I'd better go tell Jake the truth before someone talks to him."

When Nat started out the door everyone laughed, sobering as Nat turned and snapped her fingers. "By the way, I saw your two studs working on the abandoned building that Hope and Charity just bought. They're completely remodeling the inside. I think the three guys that just moved here are helping them."

Kelly nodded. "Yes, I know who you're talking about. They're brothers. Hope went to school with the youngest one, I think his name's Brett. I've heard that they like to share their women and had been stressed out about it, thought there had to be something wrong with them and they felt like freaks."

Kelly sipped her own juice. "Anyway, Hope told Brett about her and Charity's own background and about their hometown." She shrugged. "They got intrigued and wanted to see it for themselves."

Nat nodded. "When they saw how the town is, I heard they asked lots of questions and decided to move here. They mentioned to Garrett that they've worked in construction so he hooked them up with Boone and Chase."

Rachel's eyes misted at the mention of her baby's fathers and she covered her still flat stomach protectively.

Kelly jumped up when she heard a customer walk in. "They're going to be working on our new house with Boone and Chase." Pausing, she looked at the clock as she went to help the customer. "Blade's supposed to take me to lunch. He should have been here by now."

* * * *

Chase stared at Blade in shock and although he opened and closed his mouth several times, nothing came out.

"Are you sure?" He heard Boone ask the question that had been going through his own mind but had been unable to voice.

Blade nodded. "I heard them talking in the back room of Indulgences when I went to pick Kelly up for lunch." He looked at his watch. "Hell, I've got to go."

Chase finally found his voice. "Did she," he swallowed the lump in his throat. "Did she sound happy, or did she sound like she," he swallowed again, "like she didn't want it?"

Christ, this couldn't be happening again.

"What?" Blade erupted. ""You two had better get your heads out of your asses and go after your woman. Rachel's nothing like Mona. She wouldn't do that."

Chase looked up at Blade in surprise. "How did you—?"

"You two stayed drunk for weeks when you got home. You told me that story over and over while you got drunk at the club."

Chase turned to his brother, stunned. He saw the same look of shock on Boone's face.

"Listen," Blade continued. "If you're going to let what that other woman did to you keep you from the woman you both love and your baby that she's carrying, you're both stupider than I gave you credit for."

Blade opened the door and started to walk out, turning to them with a grin. "Congratulations, by the way. Now go get your woman."

* * * *

Boone climbed the stairs to Rachel's apartment over her lingerie store, his brother right behind him. He'd never been so nervous in his life.

"She doesn't need to have to keep going up and down these stairs," Chase muttered.

Boone got more nervous with each step. "She won't be. I don't care what she says, she's moving in with us tonight, and we're getting married as soon as possible." What if she wouldn't marry them? They hadn't been able to talk to her ever since that night. She shut them out at every opportunity. They wouldn't allow it again. She carried their baby, and she had to listen. He paused on the steps, and Chase almost ran into him.

"What's wrong?"

Boone grinned. "Rachel's having our baby. I still can't believe it."

Chase smiled. "I know. We should have known Rachel wouldn't be like Mona." He shook his head. "I can't believe we've been so hung up on the past that we didn't see it before."

"We're stupid all right," Boone agreed. "But I think that once we explain everything to Rachel, she'll forgive us. I hope."

Boone started back up the stairs, Chase at his heels. Knocking, he waited, going over in his mind what he wanted to say. He and Chase had tried for the last six weeks to get her to talk to them to no avail. Stubborn woman. Witch. God, he couldn't wait to hold her.

He shook his head, mentally berating himself. He and his brother had let the past cloud their judgment and had been too afraid to make a commitment. She and the baby belonged to them, and nothing would stand in their way of claiming her. He knocked harder. Now that Rachel carried their baby inside her, the choice had been taken out of their hands. He felt as though a weight had been lifted from his shoulders.

"Do you think she's in the shower?" He heard the worry in Chase's voice. "What if she fell? What if she's hurt?"

Boone tried to look in the window, but the curtain blocked his view. "Move back." Boone stepped back and charged, hitting the door with his shoulder and crashing through it. They heard her scream and shot forward to see her scrambling up on the sofa, wide-eyed in terror.

"What, what happened? What are you doing?" she stammered hoarsely.

"Are you all right?" Both men rushed to her. Boone sat on the sofa next to her and Chase knelt at her feet.

Rachel looked a little dazed as she looked at both of them. "You broke down my door!"

Boone took in her bewildered look, her flushed cheeks and his worry increased. "You didn't answer the door. We got worried. Chase and I are going to get you to the doctor, baby. Don't worry about a thing."

He wrapped her afghan securely around her as he spoke. He bent and lifted her, loving the feel of her in his arms but worried at the dark circles shadowing her eyes.

"Put me down."

As he moved to the broken door, she started to struggle. "Easy, baby. I don't want you to wiggle around while I'm on the stairs. Let's let Dr. Hansen take a look at you."

"There is nothing wrong with me, you idiot. Put me down."

Boone froze and looked down at her, then at his brother on the other side of her.

"Then why didn't you answer the door?" Chase demanded as he tucked the afghan higher.

"I was asleep."

Boone blinked. "You're really all right?"

"Except for having a broken door, I'm fine. Put me down and get out."

* * * *

Rachel fought against the erotic tingles running through her at his nearness. Being held against Boone's hard chest brought her body to life. She knew she'd always love both of them. There would always be a special connection with them, especially now that she carried their baby. But she didn't want to be with someone who didn't want her, even though her heart and body craved them both. Feeling their hands on her reminded her too much of the night they'd had together.

"Sleeping?" Boone smiled at her tenderly, and her heart leapt. He moved back to the sofa and set her gently onto the cushions. "Is our baby making you tired?"

Rachel slumped. So that's why they'd come over. "Who told you?" she asked tiredly.

Chase frowned at her tone. "It doesn't matter who told us. Why didn't *you*?"

Rachel sighed. "I would have eventually. I'm still trying to get used to the idea of being pregnant."

She refused to let herself weaken under their tender gazes. She couldn't let them get under her skin again. Or inside her, throbbing, stroking her deeply until—. She shoved the afghan aside and stood. Both men moved close, hands outstretched as if to catch her if she fell. "I'm pregnant. I'm not sick, and I'm not going to fall over."

Boone looked at her in concern. "But you fainted the other night at the store."

She didn't respond to that and walked to the kitchen to get a glass of water, turning to face them when they followed her. "Look, we have plenty of time to work out visitation rights and all that. I'm tired. I just want to fix something to eat and go to bed."

She turned to put her glass in the sink, closing her eyes against the curl of hot lust in her belly. "Now get out." She turned to face them. "I've got to call someone to fix the door."

"Sit down," Boone growled at her when she tried to brush past him. When she just glared at him, he sighed and closed his eyes, and it pricked her heart to see him looking so defeated. *Don't do it. Don't fall for it again.*

"Please, Rachel," Chase took her arm to lead her to a chair. "Please. We have something to tell you. After that, we'll fix your door and get you something to eat." He squatted down in front of her, his eyes filled with emotion. "Please, honey. We need to talk about some things."

His gaze kept flicking to her stomach.

She nodded. "Yes, I guess we need to talk." She wanted to get this over with before she did something stupid. Like cry. Or beg them to take her again. Either was a strong possibility.

Boone sat on the other side of her at the table, and she glanced at him as Chase took his seat.

"Go ahead." She folded her arms on the table and glanced at each of them expectantly. "Talk."

Boone cleared his throat. "We wanted to explain why we were so afraid of making a commitment before."

Rachel knew they didn't want a relationship with her, and she didn't feel like hearing it again.

"That's okay. I don't want a commitment from either of you anymore." She started to rise. "So if that's all—"

"Sit down," Boone growled again, then sighed heavily. "Please."

Rachel sank back into her seat. She found it nearly impossible to sit here with them like this. Seeing their hands, she remembered how good they felt on her, in her. Looking at their mouths, her heart raced, thinking about how their lips felt on hers, on her breasts, on her—

"We want you to understand," Boone said softly.

"Okay." Rachel nodded, wondering what she'd missed.

"A little more than four years ago," Boone began, his voice low and hard, "Chase and I lived with a woman named Mona. She worked in our office and made it obvious that she wanted us."

Rachel wondered if Boone knew his hands had clenched into fists as he spoke.

"She loved spending our money. She loved the attention of having two men." He paused as though remembering. "I was going through the mail one day, and found a bill for a lab test." He looked up and stared into her eyes. Rachel was shaken by the overwhelming sadness in them. "It was for a pregnancy test."

No. This couldn't be good.

Chase took up the story. "We waited to see if she would tell us about it. She didn't, and suddenly she didn't want sex any more. When a week went by and she didn't say a word about it, we confronted her."

Chase reached over and began to play with her fingers, and she couldn't help but grip his hand, hoping to comfort him. "She told us not to worry about it. She'd already had an abortion."

Rachel gasped, looking at each of them. She could only imagine how awful that must have been for them.

Chase shook his head. "Boone and I were devastated. How could she abort our baby without even discussing it with us? We told her we would have married her."

"She laughed," Boone said in a voice so raw, she winced. "She told us she only wanted the sex, said she liked fucking men two at a time, but she wasn't serious about us and didn't want a kid who had two fathers. She told us it was fun while it lasted, but she didn't want any brats."

Rachel felt tears prick her eyes at the thought of what Boone and Chase had been through. "I'm so sorry you had to go through that." She reached out to touch each of them. "Is that when you decided to come back to Desire?"

"Yeah," Chase nodded. "We sold everything and came back home." He leaned toward her and took both her hands in his. "That's why we were so afraid of commitment. We thought if we saw each other for a while, well—"

"You could test drive me," Rachel finished for him. "See what kind of woman I am. If I was only in it for the sex, you would be free and clear."

"It's not like that," Boone said through clenched teeth.

"Let me ask you both something." Rachel regarded them steadily. "How come neither of you used a condom with me? If you were that worried about an unwanted pregnancy, you would have used them."

"We forgot," Chase admitted sheepishly. "We've never had sex without one, even with Mona. We got a bad box and a few broke." He smiled tenderly at her. "You had us so worked up, all we thought about was having you. We didn't even think about it until the next day."

Boone moved from his chair to kneel in front of her. "What we're trying to say, baby, is that we've loved you for a long time but have been too stupid and scared to do anything about it. Now that you're having our baby we want you to move in with us. We'll get married as soon as it can be arranged."

Silence filled the room. A part of Rachel thrilled at the thought of being married to them. Another part of her wondered if they really did love her or if they only wanted to marry her because she'd gotten pregnant.

"Let me see if I understand you." She stood and circled the table. "You loved me but have managed to avoid me for almost two years. You didn't want to become involved with me because you thought I might be like your ex-girlfriend, who you discovered didn't love you and only wanted a ménage. And," she raised her hand to silence them when they both started to speak, "now that you know I'm pregnant with your baby, you've decided to put all that aside and marry me anyway. Maybe you want to keep an eye on me so I won't go behind your back and have an abortion?"

Boone jumped from his chair, sending it flying backward. "It's not like that, damn it! We know you're not like her. I admit, we've been stupid. But we love you, Rachel, you *and* the baby. We want to spend our lives with you, take care of you. We want lots of babies with you."

Rachel stood with her arms folded over her chest. "So if I hadn't gotten pregnant, would we still be having this conversation?"

Chase stood and approached her. "Probably not now," he admitted. "But we would have eventually." He grinned at her. "We wouldn't have been able to resist you much longer."

Rachel eyed them both warily. "I don't believe you, and I'm perfectly capable of taking care of myself and my baby. I'm going to go get something to eat from the diner. Fix my door."

Ignoring their dumbfounded looks, Rachel slipped on her shoes, grabbed her purse and headed out the broken door.

"Damn it, Rachel. This isn't over."

She heard Boone's shout as she stepped around the door, but ignored it. She needed some time alone. And she needed to get away from both of them before she did something really, really stupid. Again.

Chapter 4

Rachel climbed the stairs to her apartment, smiling when she saw the new door. Wow. They worked fast.

She blinked when she noticed the new lock. How was she supposed to get in? Hesitantly, she reached for the knob. Finding it unlocked, she walked inside. Boone sat on her sofa, apparently waiting for her, her suitcases all around him.

"I didn't see your truck. Where's Chase?" She looked around but didn't see him. "Why are my suitcases out here?"

Boone stood and crossed to her, leading her to the sofa.

"Did you have dinner?" he asked as he started to remove her shoes. "Here, put your feet up and rest until Chase gets back."

Rachel pulled her feet from his grasp as he started to lift them onto the sofa. "I don't want to put my feet up. Where's Chase and why are my suitcases out?" She began to get a sinking feeling in the pit of her stomach. "What are you two up to?"

"You're moving in with us."

"Like hell."

"I've warned you about that mouth."

"What are you going to do?" Rachel sneered. "Spank me?"

Boone's eyes darkened dangerously as he leaned toward her. When he moved to nibble at her neck, she arched it, automatically giving him access as desire shot through her. Damn. She couldn't resist him at all.

"We've already talked to the Doc. Our baby's all snug and cozy, and there are lots of other ways to punish you. Don't provoke me," he growled and tilted her face for his kiss. "Besides, I'd rather have you in my arms."

It seemed like forever since she'd felt him this way, but her body remembered him clearly. She moaned into his mouth when he deepened his kiss, sending her soaring as he took her mouth possessively with his. When he pulled her onto his lap, she melted into him, the feel of his muscled thighs beneath her bottom and the strong arms wrapped around her, making her feel unbelievably feminine and desired. His chest felt so good, a wall of heat that she snuggled into.

His erection prodding into her hip aroused her even further. She raised her arms to aid his efforts when he began to remove her shirt. Her bra quickly followed as he exposed her breasts to his gaze. His hand cupped her, and she felt her nipple harden in his palm.

"Look at you," Boone breathed. The way he looked at her made her feel like the most desired woman in the world.

Chase came through the door, grinning when he saw them. "It looks like I'm just in time." He turned to lock the door before joining them.

Boone touched a finger to a nipple and gently stroked.

"Are your nipples more sensitive, baby?"

"Yesssss," she hissed as Chase began to stroke the other.

Their eyes blazed but they touched her almost reverently, their hands gentle but thorough. And they did it so slowly she wanted to scream.

They spent a lot of time on her breasts, cupping and tracing patterns on them over and over until she thought she'd go crazy. Her shoulders tingled where their lips touched as they ran their fingers over her arms. Her thighs quivered as they stroked them, her toes curling in reaction.

Boone's mouth nipped and ate at hers hotly, hungrily. His tongue swept her mouth repeatedly, tangling with hers. She gripped his head and held him to her, moaning into his mouth. She lost herself in their touch, feeling wanton and desired, sitting topless as they devoured her. She felt Chase's mouth on her breasts and jolted when he touched a nipple.

"These nipples are really sensitive now, aren't they, honey?"

Boone lifted his mouth from hers, and they both turned to Chase.

"Yes," she panted, but couldn't say more before he lowered his mouth to hers. She released Boone to hold onto Chase as he took her mouth again and again.

She felt their hands on her breasts, teasing them too gently and making her squirm. She needed more.

When Chase lifted his head, her eyes remained closed as she absorbed the sensation of having their hands on her again. Between them, they stripped off her khakis and panties. Her pussy clenched with the need to be filled, weeping in preparation. She parted her thighs, anxious for them to touch her as her head fell back on Boone's arm.

Instead, she felt hands on her stomach and looked down to see that they each had a hand over where their baby grew, staring at her reverently.

"We made a baby," Boone choked, his eyes glittering with unshed tears.

Chase looked equally overcome with emotion, and she smiled at them tremulously, touching each of their faces. "I know. I couldn't believe it when Doc told me. Sometimes I still can't."

"We're going to take good care of you, sugar," Boone promised and touched her lips with his.

The large, rough callused hands moving over her felt gentler than she'd ever imagined they could be.

Boone's kiss soon had her flying, and being held so firmly, she felt wrapped in a cocoon of warmth. Her hand fisted on his back as the other held his head close. A hand at the back of her head held her securely for his mouth to explore hers while his other hand cupped a breast, stroking a thumb over her nipple.

She gasped into his mouth, her hands tightening on him desperately when she felt Chase spread her thighs and move to kneel between them.

Boone lifted his head, studying her expression and smiling down at her indulgently. He saw his brother lower his head and spread her folds.

"Do you know what Chase is going to do to you, baby?"

"Oh God. Yes." She cried out at the first touch of Chase's mouth on her delicate flesh, aware that Boone continued to watch her face intently. His hand continued to stroke her breast as he lowered his head, placing soft, nuzzling kisses along her jaw and down her neck.

Rachel arched eagerly to give Boone access, crying out her pleasure. Chase's tongue slid repeatedly through her slit, teasing her by flicking his tongue lightly all around her and chuckling when she tried to wiggle in their grasp.

"Chase, stop teasing me," Rachel cried out in a tortured wail.

"I'll give you what you need, sugar baby. Are you going to give us what *we* need?"

Rachel heard the hard edge of determination under the teasing tone, but ignored it. She wanted Boone's lips on hers again, but he denied her, deftly nipping and nibbling on her sensitive neck and shoulders. She thrashed, but being held like this she couldn't move at all.

"Stop struggling, baby," Boone said against her lips. "You have to be careful now."

"Then don't tease me," she gasped when Chase's tongue pressed into her.

"You are going to come home with us, baby, aren't you?" Boone asked near her ear.

"No. Please, Chase." Her clit swelled and throbbed as he continued to tease it, flicking it with his tongue just often enough to keep sending her higher, keep her juices flowing but not enough to send her over. She tried to twist away from his teasing mouth to no avail. She couldn't move closer or close her legs. His broad shoulders kept her thighs spread wide.

"Baby, we want to take care of you and the baby. We love you both very much." Boone ran a thumb back and forth over a sensitive nipple.

"No," Rachel panted. "I know you don't love me. Don't lie to me. I'll have sex with you, just don't lie to me."

"We do love you," Boone insisted, "but we know it's going to take a while for you to believe it. In the meantime, we want to take care of you. Say you'll move in with us, and Chase will give you what you want."

Chase's mouth never faltered while Boone spoke to her. Now he blew lightly on her clit, while his fingers stroked her dripping pussy, curling them inside her and making her cry out.

A flick of his tongue had her arching on Boone's lap as she cried out hoarsely. Just when she thought she'd go over, Chase removed his fingers.

"No, damn you," she wailed and used her heels to kick at his back. She grabbed Boone's shoulder and back, desperately trying to hold on.

"She's a wild one, isn't she?" Chase chuckled and lifted his head, only to lower it again.

Boone leaned down and used the flat of his tongue to lick her nipple, making her cry out again. With his head poised above her breast, Boone rumbled, his breath hot on her moist nipple. "Chase and I can do this for hours, baby." He licked her nipple again. "A man can get lost in the taste of his woman. You're our woman. While you're getting used to it, we'll give you this pleasure over and over." Boone lowered his head to suck a nipple into his mouth at the same time Chase used her own juices to lube her and began to press a finger into her bottom.

Gasping a cry, she dug her heels into Chase's back and hung on desperately to Boone.

"Your little bottom is holding on tight, sugar," Chase informed her smugly. He swept his tongue over her clit, and she felt the warning signs.

So close!

"If you come home with us, I'll take your bottom nice and slow. I'll make you come so hard, baby." Another swipe of his tongue and the feel of teeth scraping her nipple had her thrashing in their grasp, inadvertently taking Chase's blunt finger deeper. Oh! It felt so good. How had she ever survived without them?

"Yes, Rachel. You like that. Say the word, and I'll suck on your shiny little clit." Another devastating lick, a little more of his finger.

"Say it, sugar," Chase taunted.

Boone lifted his head from her breast and began nibbling at her bottom lip, his fingers poised over her nipple, holding it but not exerting any pressure.

One touch, one tiny bit more and she'd go over. So close. But they played her body well, and knew just how close she'd become. She panted and moaned helplessly. Damn it. She had to come. She couldn't stand it anymore. "Yessss," she hissed and they immediately rewarded her.

The fingers holding her nipple tightened, the thick finger in her bottom pushed deep. Chase sucked her clit into his mouth and she screamed. Her body stiffened in shock and ecstasy as her orgasm hit her with a force of a tornado. She spun out of control, lost in the storm, feeling nothing and everything as her senses whirled.

A deep underlying sense of security let her soar, safe in the knowledge that Boone and Chase would take care of her. She flew high and far before slowing, finally coming to rest and landing softly, surrounded by heat, low voices and soothing hands.

"We love you, sugar." Rachel felt Chase's lips on her abdomen, where their baby grew.

"Don't," she protested weakly. "You love the baby, not me. That's fine, just don't lie to me."

Boone lifted her to sit on his lap, holding her gently.

"Don't get upset, baby. If you want us to stop saying it for now, we will." He lifted her face to his. "But it's still true. We'll just have to convince you." He smiled tenderly. Her eyes widened when she saw that his hands shook. His erection pressed against her bottom and she knew how aroused he'd become.

She looked at the front of Chase's jeans and saw the huge bulge pressing against his zipper. He started gathering her clothes, wincing when he saw that her bra and panties had been destroyed.

"Sorry, Rach. You'll have to do without until we get home. Everything's already packed."

"Listen, maybe—" she began.

"No." Boone shook his head and stood, setting her on her feet. "You can't keep climbing up and down those stairs. What if you fell? What happens when you're too tired when you come home from work to fix something to eat?"

Boone handed her the khakis they'd removed. "We're the fathers of that baby you're carrying and it's our responsibility, *our pleasure*," he added when she would have interrupted, "to take care of both of you."

With her pants fastened, Boone helped her into her shirt. "If you don't want to talk about how we feel about you right now, we won't." He held her face in his hands. "But you're crazy if you think we're leaving you here alone or that you're going to push us out of your life."

After she slipped on her shoes and grabbed her purse, Chase turned her toward the door and swatted her bottom. "We're in your life to stay, and the sooner you get used to that, the better it will be for all of us."

Rachel stood with her hands on her hips and regarded them both steadily as they gathered her suitcases. Living with them would be like a dream come true in some ways, and a constant strain in others. She didn't trust their abrupt change of heart which only occurred when they'd learned about the baby. She hadn't lied when she'd told them that she didn't want to hear any declarations of love from them. It was hard enough dealing with her feelings for them, and now with a baby on the way, she had even more to adjust to.

"This is hard for me," she told them softly. "I'm having a baby. I have to hire help for the store now, when I'm used to taking care of it myself." She looked at them both pleadingly, her eyes begging them to understand. "Now you want me to move in with you. My whole life is changing all at once for two men who told me not too long ago that they didn't want a commitment."

"Rachel—" Boone began.

"No. I don't want to hear all about how you fell in love with me." She glared at them. "It only happened after you learned about the baby."

"Enough!" Boone dropped the suitcases and strode toward her, gripping her upper arms. "We've admitted we made a mistake with you. We compared you to someone who's nothing like you, and that was wrong. *We* were wrong." He leaned down until his face was only inches from hers. "But whether you believe us or not, we love you, *and* our baby. And we're going to take care of both of you if we have to tie you to a bed to do it." His eyes shot sparks at her as he raised a brow, all arrogant determination. "Now are you walking out to the truck or do you need to be carried? One way or the other you're going."

Rachel stared at him, angry that she felt like crying. Damned hormones. She glanced over at Chase who watched her just as intently and wore the same arrogant look as his brother.

Silence filled the room for several heartbeats, and she realized just how much she wanted to be with them. She knew they'd fight, and she'd probably regret it more than once. But she felt so tired. It would be nice to have someone to share the joys and fears of her pregnancy with on a daily basis, and who better than the men she loved and her baby's fathers? She just had to keep reminding herself not to believe they cared too much about her. She knew they felt something for her, and with a baby on the way it would be enough for now.

Lifting the strap of her purse to her shoulder, she sighed. "Did you get my prenatal vitamins and my saltines?"

Chapter 5

Rachel settled into the master bedroom of Boone and Chase's sprawling ranch house, surprised that neither man used the room themselves. "Why don't either one of you use this room? It's beautiful."

The large room had huge windows so she knew there would be plenty of light. The furniture looked heavy but the light color of the wood gave the room an open feel. A sitting area located on one side contained a sofa, two overstuffed chairs and an entertainment center. The whole room had been done in light browns and pale blue making it feel comfortable and inviting.

"This room is for sharing," Boone muttered as he dropped a suitcase on the bed. "Chase brought all the stuff you had on hangers earlier."

Chase walked in, carrying two more of her suitcases, dropped them on the floor and moved to the closet, swinging the door open. "I hung everything up. You'll probably want to rearrange it."

Rachel's eyes widened when she saw the size of the closet. "It's like another room," she exclaimed in delight.

She saw they'd installed a section for shoes and purses, another place to hang belt and scarves. "After seeing what you did at Indulgences, I shouldn't be surprised. This is wonderful!"

She could see by the look of relief on their faces that they'd wanted her approval. Noticing that they had been nervous unraveled some of her own knotted nerves. They both seemed anxious to please her, which touched her immensely.

"Everything is beautiful." She walked back to the bed and opened the first suitcase. "This bed is huge." She smiled at them teasingly. "If you can't find me, check here first. I'll probably get lost in it."

"I'm glad you like it, sugar." Chase came forward and dropped a kiss on her forehead. "We had Jared, Reese and Duncan make it for us."

Rachel just looked at him when he looked sheepish, as though he hadn't meant to reveal that. Why on earth would they have a bed specially made if they didn't plan to use it?

"Well, it's beautiful. And that bathroom." she added quickly, eager to dispel the sudden attention. "I can't wait to soak in that tub."

"Later. Why don't you come have your piece of pie while we're eating dinner?" Boone frowned. "Are you sure you're not hungry?" They'd stopped on the way home for takeout from the diner.

"No, I already ate while you fixed my door, remember? Besides, I want to get my clothes put away and get settled in." She lifted the first stack of clothes and started to put them away in the huge dresser. "Why don't you call me when you're finished with your dinner? I'll have a piece of pie with you."

Boone looked reluctant to leave. "Just don't lift any suitcases. When that one's empty, call us. One of us will put another one on the bed for you."

With the promise that she would, they left her alone to finish. Rachel took her time, loving the feel of the thick taupe carpet beneath her bare feet as she moved around the room. She could hear the men's voices in the other room and the sounds of them moving around in the kitchen. Used to being alone, somehow hearing the sounds of someone else nearby comforted her.

When she'd finished with the first suitcase, they still hadn't finished eating. Not wanting to interrupt them, she pushed another one onto its side. It made a heavy thud and she wondered how Chase had carried it in so easily. She probably wouldn't have been able to lift it. She unzipped it and heard loud footsteps tearing down the hall. She looked up in surprise.

"*Rachel*!" She heard Chase's shout as both men ran into the room, almost tripping on the suitcases.

"What's wrong?" She got to her feet. "What happened?"

"Are you okay?" Boone demanded, pulling her into his arms.

She frowned. "Of course. Why wouldn't I be?"

"She pushed the suitcase over," Chase muttered, gesturing to the one she'd just unzipped.

"I didn't lift it. I'm not stupid and I'm certainly not taking any chances of hurting the baby."

"We heard it fall and thought, oh hell." Boone scrubbed a hand over his face. "I told you to call us when you were finished." He went to the bed and removed the empty suitcase as Chase hauled the one she'd just unzipped onto the bed.

"You hadn't finished your dinner. I thought I'd just unpack it there on the floor."

"Next time call us," Chase growled.

"Why are you so nice to all the women in town and flirt with them all the time, but yell and growl at me?" Rachel demanded, hands on her hips, narrowing her eyes when he scowled at her.

"Because they don't make me crazy," he snapped. "You do."

As Rachel watched him storm from the room, her brows rose in surprise at his outburst. Looking over to where Boone silently watched her, she nervously rubbed her arms. "I've never seen Chase act like that," she murmured softly.

"Neither have I." Boone regarded her steadily. "But then, neither one of us has ever been in love before." He shrugged and started to walk out of the room, tossing over his shoulder. "I'm sure we're all going to be in for some surprises, baby."

Rachel stared at his back, not sure what he'd meant by that. They'd acted differently since finding out about the baby. Then again, she thought, placing a hand protectively over where their baby grew, this had changed all their lives. She sat on the bed, looking around again at what had become, at least for now, her bedroom.

She knew that Boone and Chase had built this house themselves. She'd known it before, had heard people rave about it. She would have had to have been blind not to have seen the pride reflected in their eyes as they showed her around. But why would they build a house like this for themselves, have a huge master bedroom and bath, with two enormous walk-in closets, but not use it? It didn't make sense.

Somewhere along the way they must have realized that they would be sharing this house with a woman. Why had they been so quick to rule out a commitment with her, damn it, if they'd already built a house to share with someone? Everything pointed to the fact that they didn't really love her. The only reason they wanted her here had to be because of the baby growing inside her. Depressed, with tears stinging her eyes, *damned hormones,* she started when her cell phone rang. Rummaging through her purse, she finally found it and blinking away tears, answered.

"Hello?"

"Rach, how do you feel about selling me half the lingerie shop?"

Rachel couldn't prevent a smile. Her sister, Erin, never had much use for pleasantries.

"Hello, Erin. How are you?" she asked deliberately.

"I'm fine, sweetie. How are *you*?"

"I'm fine, Erin. I was going to call you tomorrow." Rachel paused and took a deep breath before blurting, "I've moved in with Boone and Chase." Rachel winced and moved the phone several inches away from her ear as the screaming began.

"I quit my job. I'm moving out there. *I'll* take care of you. You don't need those good for nothing..."

Rachel sat on the bed as the tirade continued, glancing up to see Chase standing in the doorway, his eyebrows shooting up when he heard the loud yelling coming from the phone. He strode toward her, reaching for the phone, but Rachel pulled it away.

"Who the hell is that?" he growled.

Rachel sighed. "My sister."

"You tell those two assholes you don't need their help. I'll be there in a few days."

Chase blinked when he heard Erin's voice come through loud and clear. "Jesus, Rachel. What the hell did you tell her?"

Rachel waved him away, sighing when he ignored her. "Erin!" she yelled into the phone. It took a while to get her sister calmed down. "Listen. If you want to move out here and buy half the business, that would be great, but you don't *need* to. I'm fine. I promise. I'm staying here with Boone and Chase for a while. If you really want to move here you can have my apartment. Of course I want you around."

Rachel rubbed her forehead where a headache had started.

"I know, Erin, but you don't *have* to move out here. I'm fine, honest."

Rachel knew that Chase unashamedly eavesdropped on her conversation.

"If you're sure that's what you want to do. No, you can't talk to them."

She blinked as Chase ripped the phone out of her hand.

"Hello. This is Chase."

Rachel groaned when she heard her sister's raised voice again, afraid of what Chase would say to her.

Five years older than her, Erin had always taken her position as big sister seriously, especially after their parents had been killed by a drunk driver while they'd still been in their teens. Erin, at eighteen, had suddenly become responsible for her thirteen-year-old sister.

When Rachel had told Erin about her pregnancy, Erin had tried to get her to come live with her in Houston. Rachel had turned her down, explaining that she had a business and a life here in Desire that she didn't want to leave.

Now, her sister had quit her job as a secretary in a big oil company to come here. If Chase dared to yell at her sister, she would leave so fast his head would spin. Erin had become more mother than sister and had sacrificed too many times for her already. She didn't need Erin's help but her sister wouldn't be swayed.

"Yes ma'am," she heard him say. "You're absolutely right. My brother and I both acted like idiots, but we smartened up in a hurry."

When Boone walked in and looked curiously at Chase, then at her, she whispered, "It's my sister, Erin."

He nodded and motioned to Chase that he wanted the phone when Chase had finished.

"Yes ma'am. We are trying to talk her into marrying us, but so far she won't."

When Chase laughed, Rachel couldn't help smiling in amusement as he tried to work his charm on her sister, not an easy thing to do.

"Yes ma'am. I'm looking forward to meeting you in person. You've done a good job raising your sister, and if she's anything like you, Boone and I will have to spend all our time beating the single men of Desire off of you."

Whenever Erin said made Chase laugh again.

"Yes, ma'am. Call us when you get close." He rattled off his and Boone's cell numbers. "Yes, ma'am. He standing right here waiting to talk to you. We'll see you in a few days."

Chase handed Boone the phone and turned to Rachel. "Come on. Let's go have some pie."

"But..." Rachel protested as Chase led her from the room.

"Don't worry. Boone can handle your sister."

When Boone joined them several minutes later, he had a big smile on his face. "Erin will be here sometime next week." He dropped a kiss on Rachel's pie filled mouth and straightened, licking his lips. "Mmm, apple. My favorite."

She frowned when he poured a glass of milk and placed it in front of her. "I don't like milk. I usually have herbal tea," she protested.

"Too bad. We don't have any herbal tea and both you and the baby need milk," Boone told her. He sipped his coffee before taking a bite of his own pie.

"You're bossy," she complained. She sipped the milk. If they would all be living here together she knew she would have to pick her battles.

"That's a given," Boone agreed and took another bite of the pie.

Rachel finished her pie and milk as the conversation turned to the books they'd bought on pregnancy. Rachel stared at them dumbfounded as they talked about what they'd read so far.

"Well, they were right about her nipples being more sensitive." Boone nodded. "We have to be more careful not to hurt her."

Chase leered at her. "I'll practice again in a little while."

"I'm going to go take a bath," she told them both crossly, angry at the way her nipples had already puckered. It didn't seem fair that they could arouse her so easily. She'd love to be able to blame it on pregnancy hormones but she had always been this way with them. One intense look from them and her body came alive. They only had to glance at her breasts and they swelled, her nipples pebbling and standing up for their attention. One dark rumble of their voices promising some erotic pleasure had her panties soaked and her stomach tightening with need.

Bastards. They knew what they did to her. One day soon she wanted to beat them at their own game.

"Go take your bath, baby." Boone's smile promised erotic delight. "We'll clean this up and take a quick shower and then we'll be right there."

Rachel lifted her chin. "I'm going to bed."

"Not alone." Chase stood and took their dishes to the sink. "Go soak in the tub, sugar. You'll feel better."

"Don't tell me what to do!"

"You're the one who said you wanted to take a bath," Boone pointed out.

Rachel glared at him. "I know what I said."

"Okay." Boone agreed patiently.

"Ohhhh," Rachel stomped her foot and stormed out, even more angry when she heard Boone say to his brother, "hormones".

* * * *

Rachel had unpacked her bath things earlier, arranging them the way she wanted around the tub. She started filling the oversized tub, adding a liberal amount of the raspberry bath oil she liked. When she went back into the bedroom to gather her nightgown and put her hair up in a clasp, she heard the other showers running. Damn, they'd straightened the kitchen already.

They could wait. She wouldn't rush through her bath. She undressed and dropped her clothes in the hamper, making a mental note to run a load of clothes through the washer before she went to work the next day. She'd better take over doing the laundry. There was no telling what would happen to her delicate bras and panties if Boone and Chase tried to wash them.

She stepped into the round tub and lowered herself into the scented warm water, moaning in bliss as she settled, leaning back against the side. She'd rolled a towel and used it to pillow her head and closed her eyes as the tub continued to fill.

Rachel had almost fallen asleep when she heard the water being turned off, and she opened one eye.

"Go away," she slurred sleepily and closed her eye again.

"Nope." Chase laughed softly. "We came to give you a bath. Besides, if we left, you'd probably drown."

"I can take a bath all by myself," Rachel told him without opening her eyes. She would not look at him again. The brief glance she'd had of him wearing nothing but his boxers had been enough to make her pulse speed up. She hoped he'd attribute her pebbled nipples to the air touching them, cool compared to the bath water. Since she sat in the tub, he wouldn't know about the moistening that had started between her legs.

"We know you can, baby." Boone's voice came from directly behind her and had her eyes popping open to see him leaning over her from behind. "But we want to give you your bath. Just lie back and enjoy it," he told her when she struggled to sit up. Damn, so much for ignoring them.

Boone's strong hands on her shoulders settled her back down into the warm water.

"I'm going to smell like raspberries, but what the hell." Chase laughed. Stepping out of his boxers, he joined her in the tub. "That's better. Now I can reach everything."

Rachel got a good look at his cock as he stepped into the tub and her stomach fluttered. The large, plum sized head glistened, and her pussy clenched hungrily. He soaped a loofah with her raspberry soap before passing the soap to Boone.

"I can't even take a bath in peace," she complained, then ruined it by moaning in pleasure as Boone's soapy hands covered her breasts.

She watched Chase's cock play peek-a-boo as it bobbed in the water, and she stifled a groan.

"Does that feel good, baby?"

"Mmm hmm." When she felt Boone's lips on her neck and shoulder Rachel tilted her neck to give him better access. His soapy hands continued to move over her chest and stomach, moving back to her breasts frequently to play with her nipples.

She absorbed the feel of Boone surrounding her. She laid her head on his shoulder as both of his arms came around her. His slippery hands moving over her breasts felt hot as did his mouth on her neck and shoulder.

Chase spread her thighs and sat between them, lifting a foot to his chest, and began to soap her leg. The muscles of his chest bunched and flexed under her foot. He drew the loofah lightly over her skin over and over, gradually working his way up her thigh. She pressed her foot harder against his chest to lift herself, holding her breath when he moved it between her legs, allowing the rough loofah to barely skim over her slit. Gasping, she lifted into it but Chase chuckled and moved it away.

"None of that. This is too rough for that soft little pussy."

Boone washed her arms, tickling her underarms as Chase moved to the other leg.

"You used the bath oil in here, didn't you?" Boone asked, gesturing to one of the bottles on the rim of the tub.

"Yes," Rachel moaned when he lifted her rinsed arms to circle his neck, effectively lifting her breasts for his hands.

"I don't want you to use that anymore unless one of us is with you. You could slip and fall." Boone's voice sounded low but firm, the voice she'd learned that meant arguing would be pointless. She didn't feel like arguing anyway as their hands worked their magic on her body.

"Okay," she whispered on a moan as his slippery hands covered her breasts again, while his mouth continued to play havoc with her senses, moving over her neck and shoulders, kissing and nibbling at the sensitive skin there.

Chase again worked his way to her now needy slit.

They both spoke softly to her, loving her with their words as they did with their hands. As their touch became more intimate, their words became more erotic.

"Look at how these pretty breasts fit in my hands," Boone said, flicking his thumbs over her nipples.

Chase dropped the loofah and reached down and spread her folds with his thumbs, capturing her clit between them. Boone supported her shoulders when Chase lifted her from the water and scooted forward until her bottom rested on his thighs. She rocked on him as he rubbed her clit between his thumbs. "Look how red this clit is."

"Do you remember what I told you I would do to you if you came home with us?" Chase asked silkily.

"Oh God, yes." Rachel groaned and her bottom clenched in response.

"What a good girl," Boone crooned to her, his voice rumbling in her ear and making her shiver. "You left the massage oil right where we could reach it. Is it raspberry, too?"

"Yesss," Rachel hissed. Chase pushed a finger inside her wet pussy, stroking while Boone rinsed the soap from her chest and lightly pinched her nipples. Her body trembled at their touch, moving on Chase's finger. His eyes shot gold sparks as he watched her body respond to their teasing.

"You are so beautiful," he whispered. He looked up at Boone. "I can't wait anymore and she's getting ready to come."

Both men moved, Chase slipping out from under her thighs, while Boone raised her until she sat up in the tub. She looked over her shoulder at him, her stomach clenching at the need she saw on his face. He quickly shucked his boxers and stepped into the tub, lowering to sit on the side. His thick length looked hard and hungry, bobbing against his stomach as his body reacted to her stare. Eagerly, she turned to face him and bent, licking him from base to tip with the flat of her tongue. His answering hiss turned her on even more, and she held onto his thighs and did it again.

"Baby, you're killing me," he groaned.

"You don't like it?" She looked up at him innocently.

"I like it too much," he groaned as she did it again. "Stop teasing me, witch. Suck me."

Rachel firmed her hold on his thighs as Chase lifted her bottom, positioning her on her knees in the tub. She continued to tease Boone, kissing and licking his angry looking cock as Chase began to oil her puckered opening.

"Remember what I promised you, Rachel?" he asked tauntingly. "I'm going to take your ass nice and slow." He slid a finger inside her bottom, pressing the oil deep, his strokes slow and even.

"Faster," she demanded as she continued to tease Boone.

Boone's hands tightened on her hair. "Take me into your mouth, baby. Right now."

Rachel thrilled at the raw command. His voice rumbled low and gravelly, the way it sounded when he hung onto control by a thread. It sent a pool of lust straight to her slit, and she could feel even more moisture flow from her.

"No more rough stuff while our baby's inside you," Chase drawled. "All of our lovin's gonna be nice and slow until our baby's born."

Rachel groaned. If they planned to love her this way for the next several months, she didn't know if she would be able to survive it.

Chase poised the tip of his cock against her puckered opening and began to push inside. His hands on her hips and Boone's on her hair prevented her from pushing back on him.

Held immobile, she panted and groaned as Chase continued to press into her a millimeter at a time until the large head opened her, passing the tight ring of muscle, remaining poised just inside her. Rachel tried to squirm to no avail as Chase stopped, not pushing any further.

She lifted her mouth from Boone's cock. "More," she growled over her shoulder at Chase.

"If you want my cock pushed all the way in your ass, you'd better start sucking Boone." Chase's voice sounded raw with need as he held himself still. "Stop teasing Boone, sugar. Suck him good, and I'll fuck your ass deep."

Rachel needed no further encouragement. The time for play had ended, and she needed to have Boone's cock in her mouth. Taking him to her throat in one stroke, she used her tongue on the sensitive underside and began sucking him in earnest. He rewarded her immediately with a hoarse cry, and his thighs tightened beneath her hands.

"Oh yes, baby. Jesus, that mouth is incredible," Boone panted.

"You keep working on Boone's cock, sugar, while I work on your ass."

Rachel sucked Boone's thick cock frantically as Chase pressed steadily into her.

"Christ, the way she's clenching on me," Chase groaned as he continued to press his length into her. "It feels like her ass is sucking me in."

"Damn, that's beautiful," Boone groaned, and Rachel knew he watched not only her mouth on him but also Chase's cock disappearing into her ass.

It increased her pleasure to know that she could please them both this way. She knew their pleasure doubled as Boone got pleasure not only from her mouth on his cock, but also from watching Chase take her ass. She knew Chase's pleasure came from not only fucking her ass, but watching her suck Boone.

Rachel heard Boone's harsh growls and muffled curses and knew his control was gone. His cock pulsed in her mouth and she heard his hoarse cry as he spurted his seed down her throat. She swallowed repeatedly, eliciting more harsh groans from him. His hands swept over her back as she licked him clean while Chase continued to press until his entire length became fully imbedded inside her.

"Oh God," she whimpered, laying her head on Boone's thigh.

"Hold onto her," Boone ordered his brother and slid into the tub beneath her, pillowing her head on his shoulder.

"Feel good, baby?" Boone asked when Chase began his slow strokes.

"It's too slow," Rachel gasped as Chase pressed deep inside her again.

"Nice and slow, baby. Remember?" Boone crooned against her forehead as he wrapped an arm around her, anchoring her securely against him.

Her hands tightened on him when she felt his other hand slip over her stomach and lower, and his fingers slipped between her folds. Chase's cock in her bottom felt as hard as steel and so hot it burned inside her. He felt huge, much larger than she thought she could bear, wider than she remembered, but still she wanted more. She couldn't keep from clenching on him. It burned each time but her body now craved it. She shivered at the full erotic feel of having him in her bottom.

When Boone unerringly found her throbbing clit, Rachel cried out and tightened on Chase in reaction.

"Fuck," Chase breathed through clenched teeth. "Even this slow I can't last with her. Push her over, damn it!"

As soon as Chase made his demand, Boone's strokes became more deliberate, and she soon raced toward an orgasm. She tingled all over, quivering under his hands. Turning her face against Boone's chest, she cried out, gripping his biceps.

He stroked her clit with expert precision. Combined with Chase's deep strokes in her bottom had her jerking and twisting and crying out as she came, water sloshing all around them. She screamed into Boone's chest, feeling the burn in her bottom as she tightened hard on Chase's steely length. His answering roar accompanied the pulsing inside her as he spilled his seed deep.

It took several minutes for them to stop shuddering and catch their breath enough to move. Rachel eventually became aware that the water had cooled. Chase pulled from her and gently cleaned her and Boone lifted her into his arms and stood, stepping out of the tub. "Come on, baby. I don't want you to catch a chill."

Boone dried her thoroughly and carried her to the bed where he tucked her in, adjusting the covers around her.

"Good night, baby." Boone slid in beside her and pillowed her head on his shoulder.

"I forgot my saltines," she mumbled sleepily, and started to rise.

"Stay there, baby. Chase will get them for you."

"What does she want?" Chase asked, coming out of the bathroom.

"Her crackers," Rachel heard Boone whisper as though from a distance and tried to stay awake.

When she felt Chase slip into the bed behind her, she felt warm all over. Content and spent, she fell asleep with her head on Boone's shoulder and Chase pressed against her back, his hand warm on her hip.

Chapter 6

Rachel woke the next morning afraid to move. Taking deep breaths, she tried to keep the nausea at bay, praying she wouldn't disgrace herself by being sick all over Boone and Chase.

When Boone shifted to lean over her, she groaned. "Don't move," she whispered weakly. Seconds later she felt one of her precious saltines against her lips and chewed it gratefully.

She saw the worried looks on their faces as she finished one cracker and they offered another. By the time she'd finished three of them, she had started to feel better.

"You okay, Rachel?" Chase asked worriedly when she refused another cracker.

"I'm okay now, thanks." She sat up gingerly, waiting to see if the nausea had truly passed. "I'm sorry about that. I was afraid I was going to be sick all over you before I could climb over one of you to get up."

Boone touched her lips tenderly with his. "It's our baby that's making you sick to your stomach. Don't worry about that, baby. We're all in this together."

Rachel blushed and nodded, starting to realize how intimate sharing this pregnancy with them would be.

* * * *

Over the next several days, she came to realize just how intimate.

Every morning she woke, greeted with saltines. Both men stayed with her until her nausea had passed. Knowing she wouldn't be able to handle breakfast, at least for a while, they took her to work only to reappear an hour later with breakfast, then later for lunch.

They wanted to know everything she'd eaten during the day, how she felt, did she feel tired or dizzy? Had she taken her vitamin? Had she been drinking milk? They made her crazy by checking her nipples every day, inspecting them thoroughly, fascinated by the changes. This of course led to further inspection of her body and before long they'd forgotten about inspecting her and focused on pleasuring her.

Going to the grocery store made her laugh and at the same time tested her patience as they filled the cart with 'all the things a pregnant woman should eat'.

Just because she now ate for two, they assumed she should eat as much as they did, glaring at her when she said she'd had enough to eat. They constantly brought her glasses of milk, fruit juice and cups of herbal tea now stored in a jar in their kitchen. When she sat on the sofa at night to read, they lifted her feet onto the cushions, whether she wanted them there or not, massaging them as they read books on pregnancy.

Okay, she really got into the foot massages and looked forward to them. They constantly talked about marriage, which she ignored and made love to her every night, which she reveled in.

One afternoon, the week after she'd moved in, Chase walked through the door of her lingerie store, handed her a banana and cupped the back of her head, lowering his lips to hers, oblivious to the customers and their amusement. Rachel's eyes closed, and she moaned as he teased her, moving his lips lightly over her own, darting his tongue out to trace them. She growled at his teasing and grabbed the front of his shirt to yank him closer. She felt him smile against her lips before nipping her bottom lip and giving her what she wanted. She moaned into his mouth as it took hers, making her forget customers, merchandise and everything else except the way his kiss made her feel.

"That's what got her into trouble," Nat laughed.

Another giggle followed. "I see what you mean about them."

Chase lifted his head and smiled as he took in Rachel's faraway expression, before turning to look over his shoulder.

"If you ladies don't behave, I'm going to have to have a talk with your husbands."

Nat and Isabella looked at each other and burst out laughing. "You're going to have to do better than that, honey, if you're trying to intimidate us." Isabella patted him on the arm as she looked at Rachel.

Chase saw Rachel's face burn at the older woman's stare.

Isabel sighed "I used to blush like that."

"Yeah, me too." Nat laid her purchases on the counter. "What happened to those days?"

Chase looked pointedly at the items both women had placed on the counter. "When I tell your husbands what bad girls you've been, I wouldn't be a bit surprised if they ripped those lacy little panties right off, flipped you over their laps and spanked your bottoms until they blushed really nicely."

When both Nat and Isabella turned bright red, Chase chuckled and nodded, satisfied. "And there they are."

Isabella tried and failed to look stern. "You are a bad boy, Chase Jackson."

"Yes, ma'am." He smiled wickedly.

Rachel blushed even redder as she rang up their purchases. When they left, she turned to Chase. "So what are you doing here this time of the afternoon?" she asked as she peeled the banana.

* * * *

"I, uh, oh yeah, Erin's almost here."

Rachel didn't let on that she knew how he watched the way she nibbled at the tip of the fruit. "So, Erin's on her way?" He stared at her mouth as she purposely used the flat of her tongue to lick the banana.

"Uh, huh," he murmured, never taking his eyes from her mouth.

"So is the work on Hope and Charity's building almost done?" Rachel enjoyed herself immensely. The fact that she had to repeat the question tickled her even more.

"Uh, huh," he finally answered.

She glanced down to see that the bulge behind his zipper had grown as he watched her. Out of the corner of her eye, she saw Boone come in, but Chase didn't appear to notice. Lowering her mouth over the top of the banana, she hummed her appreciation and watched Chase swallow hard.

"Hi, baby." Boone kissed her forehead as she bit off a piece of banana and chewed.

Chase appeared to snap out of it and glared at her. "Very funny."

Boone looked from one to the other in confusion. "Did I miss something?"

Rachel shrugged innocently and took another bite. "I don't know what's wrong with him." She shrugged again.

Boone stared at a glaring Chase as he watched her. Perversely, she closed her mouth around the top of the banana suggestively before taking another bite.

Chase pointed at her. "See that!"

When Boone turned back to her and looked at her in confusion, she shrugged again innocently as she chewed. "He's your brother," she told him when she swallowed.

Boone gave his brother a 'what's wrong with you' look and leaned into Rachel. His mouth covered hers and he licked her lips. "Mmm, smells like raspberry, tastes like banana." He leaned down to nuzzle her neck, his voice a deep rumble in her ear. "I wonder what other delicious flavors I can find."

Rachel moaned and leaned into him, pressing her breasts against his chest.

"Those hard little nipples look and taste like little raspberries." His voice dropped lower and he bit her earlobe as his hand trailed down her body to cover her mound. "I'll bet I know where I can find some sweet honey." He cupped her head as he slid his fingers between her legs. "Are you wet, baby? Is that honey flowing?"

"Yes, damn you. Don't do this now." She tried to push away, but the rock hard wall she pressed against didn't so much as budge. "Anybody could walk in," she protested weakly as his fingers pressed harder.

"Chase is watching, baby." He turned her toward the counter, his breath hot on her ear. "Bend over the counter. I want my mouth on you."

"Boone," she protested weakly. Chase stood across the counter and leaned down to kiss her. His mouth moved hungrily on hers while Boone knelt behind her and lifted her dress. The sound of her panties being ripped off sounded loud in her ears.

"Damn it," she groaned when Chase lifted his head. "Stop ripping all my panties."

Chase bit her lip playfully as his hands covered her breasts. "Then stop wearing them." He grinned.

She felt her bottom cheeks being parted and jerked in surprise. When she tried to straighten, Chase let go of her breasts to grip her upper arms, effectively holding her in place as Boone nipped her bottom cheek.

"Oh God," she whimpered.

"What's Boone doing to you, sugar?"

"He's, he's, oohhh." Rachel gripped Chase's arms tightly.

"What's Boone doing, Rachel?" Chase reached over to pinch a nipple. "Tell me."

"He's lick,-licking my bottom," she finally managed to say.

"Is he licking that little hole that I fucked last night?" Chase's voice sounded low and gritty.

"Yessss," Rachel hissed.

"Do you like it?" Chase asked silkily.

"He can't do that." Rachel closed her eyes against such a forbidden sensation.

"Apparently he can." Chase chuckled and ate at her lips again. Chase's mouth teased and demanded, cajoled and possessed, absorbing her moans and whimpers. He cupped her head in his hand, holding her tilted exactly how he wanted her to devour her mouth with his. Nips at her lips had them tingling before he bathed them with his tongue to soothe the sting. His hand on her neck caressed, using his thumb to stroke her jaw and keep her face lifted to his.

Boone moved, shifting to sit in front of her and between her legs, his shoulders under her thighs, holding her up while his mouth ate at her slit. His hands on her bottom held her firmly in place.

Rachel groaned into Chase's mouth at the first swipe of Boone's tongue on her slit. She was glad he held her up, because she would have already collapsed as he used his mouth to lick her all over.

He teased her mercilessly, his tongue pushing inside her over and over before moving back up to lick her folds. His mouth burned hot and hungry on her, almost savage. He nipped at her thighs, and she trembled as the delicate skin became highly sensitized, the slight pang traveling straight to her pussy, making it weep even more.

Chase lifted her head, and she opened her eyes to find his stare on her. He held her head up and tilted, watching her face as Boone's mouth drove her higher and higher. Chase cupped her face, running his thumb back and forth over her cheek. "You are so beautiful, sugar. I love seeing you like this."

"Please," she begged. Oh God, she couldn't take any more.

Chase covered her breasts with his hands once again and spoke to his brother. "Finish her off."

Rachel's eyes fluttered closed as Boone's lips closed around her clit. When he sucked hard at the throbbing bundle of nerves, Rachel cried out as her orgasm hit her. She would have fallen if Boone's hands hadn't been supporting her.

Chase cupped her face, his own only inches away. He held her gaze as she came, his eyes turning gold as they held hers, not allowing her to look away. She cried out as the wave after wave of pleasure swept through her.

Boone slowed his assault, dragging out her orgasm as Chase watched her. When Boone rose and moved to stand behind her, wrapping in arm around her waist, she slumped weakly against him. "You taste incredible, baby. I want some more of that sweet honey when we get you home."

"Oh God," Rachel closed her eyes weakly. She couldn't be around them and not be aroused, and every time she found herself alone with them, they made her come. Day, night, afternoon. At home, in their truck, now in the store. Sometimes she felt like that's all she did. How could a woman fight against that?

The sound of the door opening had her straightening. Boone let go but kept a large hand on her hip. She leaned against him, grateful for his steadying presence.

Rachel smiled as Kelly came in followed by Blade.

As they approached, she saw Kelly frown over her shoulder at her adoring husband. Rachel smiled when Blade merely raised a brow at his wife, completely unperturbed.

Kelly huffed and marched up to the counter, ignoring him. "Hi everybody. Rachel, are you okay? You look kind of flushed." Kelly reached out to touch Rachel's cheek.

Rachel felt her face burn.

Blade laughed. "Rachel's fine, love. Do your shopping."

Of course *he* would know what a woman who just had a mind-blowing orgasm looked like.

Kelly's face reddened as the implications set in.

"Oh! Well then. Rachel, let's leave the men alone. Come help me pick out some new panties."

Rachel rounded the counter and started to lead Kelly away. Her knees felt like jelly and she felt like everyone in the store knew she didn't have any panties on. Well, half of them did. "Didn't you just buy a whole bunch of them?" Rachel asked softly.

Kelly looked back to glare at her husband and raised her voice enough to carry. "*Somebody* keeps ripping them."

Rachel hid a smile when Blade retorted, "Then stop wearing them around me."

* * * *

A little over an hour later, Boone and Chase stood around the table in her small kitchen, mapping out the new organizers they wanted to build for the store. Rachel watched them discuss it then go back out to the store to take measurements as she went about her business. Curiosity finally got the best of her, and she walked over to see what they'd drawn.

"But this takes up the whole wall."

Boone's brows went up. "Is that a problem? You'll be able to fit a lot in here but if you don't want it taking up that much space.—"

"It's not that," Rachel sighed. "It's just that right now I can't afford something that big. Isn't there any way to make something smaller that can be added on to?" Rachel stared down at the plans. They'd drawn in plenty of drawers and a place to display what each one contained. They'd even included little knobs to hang hangers for her to showcase some of the bras. Having something like this would certainly free up a lot of space for her other lingerie items.

Realizing they'd been silent too long, she looked up to find them both staring at her. "What's wrong?"

"You really don't think you're paying for this, do you?" Chase asked incredulously.

Rachel blinked. "Of course I'm going to pay for it. I wouldn't have asked you to—"

"Shut up, Rachel, before you dig your hole any deeper." Boone lifted a hand to cut her off when she opened her mouth to speak. "You and the baby are ours. We take care of what's ours. This is a small thing for us to do for you. We just want to make sure we haven't forgotten anything. Now," he lowered his voice, "do you like it or do you want something changed?"

Boone had used that 'Don't argue with me, you're going to lose' voice so Rachel just sighed. "It's beautiful," she told them honestly. "I really appreciate the two of you doing this for me."

"Really?" Chase looked intrigued and leaned closer. "How much do you appreciate it?"

Rachel smiled. "A lot." She knew that look well. It caused her stomach to flutter. The need for them, always simmering just below the surface rose swiftly, and her pulse raced at his suggestive look.

Chase leered. "Would you like to show us just how much you appreciate it?"

Rachel laughed even as the lust flared to life. "I thought you said I didn't have to pay for it," she mocked.

She trembled when Chase moved behind her and closed his hands over her breasts and leaned down to whisper against her neck. "We don't want your money, sugar. But we might be willing to accept another kind of payment." His voice made her break out in goose bumps as she automatically leaned back against him. "We want to know just how far you're willing to go to show us your appreciation."

"So this is how my baby sister got into trouble."

They all spun. Rachel grinned and flew across the store to where Erin stood just inside the door.

"Erin," she cried happily and flung herself at her sister.

Taller than Rachel and slightly thinner, Erin had the same brown hair and blue eyes. But while Rachel's hair curled, Erin's fell in soft waves past her shoulders and gleamed with red highlights.

Erin's arms tightened around her as Boone and Chase strode up from behind. "Damn it, Rachel. Don't run like that," Boone growled at her before greeting her sister. "Hi. I'm Boone Jackson, and this is my brother Chase."

Her sister shook hands with them, and Rachel groaned internally when Erin released her to cross her arms over her chest, glaring at them.

"Erin—" Both Boone and Chase lifted a hand to silence her.

"We want to hear whatever it is that your sister needs to say to us," Boone told her, glancing at her briefly before turning his attention back to Erin.

"Which one of you is the father of my future niece or nephew?" Erin demanded.

Chase frowned at her. "We both are."

Erin narrowed her eyes at them. "Rachel tells me that the two of you share her. Is that true?"

Boone nodded. "Yes ma'am."

"Why?"

Oh God. She should have known Erin would do this. "Erin—"

"My brother and I both love your sister," Chase began. "We've always shared women, but we never fell in love until we met Rachel."

Rachel watched nervously as Erin regarded both men. "According to Rachel, there is a lot of that in this town. Do the men in this town have a lot of trouble pleasing a woman on their own?"

Chase and Boone roared with laughter, and Erin narrowed her eyes at them. "No ma'am," Chase chortled.

Rachel felt her face burn as Erin looked over at her. "That good, huh?" She turned back to the men. "Are either one of you going to marry her?"

"Yes."

"No," Rachel said.

Erin scowled at her sister's answer. "Why don't you want to marry one of them?"

Rachel ignored the men's dark looks. "I'm not getting married."

Erin ignored that and turned back to the men. "You both can't marry her, you know."

"She'll legally be married to me," Boone told her. "The oldest male is the one that marries the woman they share but everyone already knows that she belongs to both of us."

Erin eyed Chase. "What if you decide to get married in the future?"

Chase's face tightened. "I'd consider myself just as married to Rachel as my brother. I don't cheat."

Erin regarded him for several long seconds. Apparently satisfied with what she saw, she turned back to Rachel.

"So why won't you marry them?"

Rachel glared over to where Boone and Chase stood with their arms folded over their chests, smiling smugly, obviously realizing that Erin had become their ally on the subject of marriage.

"They don't love me," Rachel told her sister. "They only want to marry me because of the baby."

"They're liars?" Erin gasped in mock horror.

"No. I didn't say that." Rachel avoided looking at Boone and Chase's smug faces.

"Sure you did," Erin replied easily. "They just told me, right to my face, that they love you. Are you telling me that it's not true?"

Rachel sighed. "They only think they love me. It's really just because of the baby."

Erin nodded wisely. "So they're stupid."

Rachel opened her mouth to deny it and saw the looks of glee on the men's faces. "Yeah, that's right. They are."

Rachel smiled when the looks of superiority became glares of promised retribution.

Erin laughed. "Good to know. But they do have big bulging muscles, and I need some help with my things."

Chapter 7

Thanks to Boone and Chase's help, the next two busy weeks passed by smoothly. They helped Erin move all of her belongings into Rachel's old apartment above the lingerie store. They moved furniture, putting everything just the way Erin wanted it and did everything they could to help her get settled. During this time her sister and her lovers got to know each other better. Boone and Chase both soon became very protective of their future sister-in-law.

One night after dinner, Boone and Chase got into a conversation with Erin about the town and the rules that people lived by in Desire.

For the first time in Rachel's life she saw her sister speechless.

"Let me get this straight," Erin managed when she finally found her voice. "The two of you consider yourselves my protectors?"

Chase grinned at her. "Yes ma'am."

Erin laughed. "I don't need anybody to protect me. Thanks anyway."

They all sat on the deck of the house Boone, Chase and Rachel shared. The nights had started getting cool, and Boone moved to adjust the throw over Rachel's feet.

"You don't have a choice," he told Erin as he lifted Rachel's feet to his lap and began massaging them.

Rachel winced when Erin glared at him.

"Excuse me?" Rachel heard Erin ask in a steely voice. Uh oh. She knew that voice well. It meant Erin's temper simmered just below the surface. She'd seen that temper often enough to respect it, something she knew her men would soon learn.

"You heard me just fine," Boone retorted, apparently unfazed by the fire in Erin's eyes. "The founders of this town made it a priority to assure that women who live here are protected. With some women having more than one husband, they thought it important that all women of Desire should be protected at all costs."

Rachel looked over at Boone, taken aback at the vehemence in his tone.

"Our town never would have grown into what it is now without a good set of rules," he continued. "We *all* live by these rules or we don't live here at all." He glanced at Erin pointedly.

"That's ridiculous," Erin scoffed. "I certainly don't need somebody to protect me. I've taken care of myself *and* Rachel since I turned eighteen."

"Until now." Chase's tone was serious. "Any man in town will move to protect you, but Boone and I are the ones who will watch you more closely. And if you do anything, *anything*," Chase added, leaning forward, "to jeopardize your own safety, Boone and I have every right to put you over our knee and spank your ass red."

"What?"

Rachel hid a grin when Erin flew out of her chair, almost knocking her wine glass over in the process. "If you think, for one minute, I'm going to let you—"

"We won't ask for permission," Boone told her in a deceptively mild voice.

"That is," Chase added tauntingly, "until somebody claims you. Of course, they'd have to come to Boone and me to do that."

Erin paled then turned red and reached for her wine glass. Guzzling its contents, she dropped back into her chair. Her eyes shot daggers at both of them. "Explain what you just said."

Rachel noticed that they both still appeared unfazed. Amazing.

"Well if somebody wants to claim you for his or their own, they'd come to Boone and me, respecting our position as your protectors."

Chase grinned at her. "A firecracker like you will have them beating down our door in no time."

Erin blanched. "I do not need a man in my life."

"That's up to you." Chase shrugged. "But until another man or men claim you and you accept their claim, you're our responsibility."

Rachel sat calmly sipping her juice as Erin glared at her. Her usually unflappable sister looked a little rough around the edges.

Erin's hand shook, almost spilling her wine. She'd paled once again as her eyes darted back and forth between Boone and Chase.

She turned to Rachel. "What have you gotten us into?"

Rachel winced. Just because she loved the town didn't mean her sister would. "You don't have to stay," she told Erin softly. "If you don't like it here..."

"You'd be willing to leave?" Erin asked.

"Rachel isn't going anywhere," Boone growled. "If you choose to leave, we can't stop you, but we can and will stop Rachel. We want you to stay, Erin, very much. But if you do, you'll have to abide by the rules of Desire." He regarded her steadily. "The rules are there for a reason, and they've worked for over a hundred years. You're not going to change them."

A short while later, Rachel looked on worriedly as Chase escorted a very subdued Erin to his truck to take her home.

* * * *

The next week Rachel and Erin happily showed their new employee around the store.

Marissa Mallory was a petite, friendly young woman with a shiny mop of blonde curls. Her striking green eyes shot with gold usually brimmed with happiness, especially when she talked about her son.

Two years old Sammy looked a lot like his mother. He wore a cap of golden curls like hers, but his eyes were a little darker, more brown than green.

She'd answered Rachel's ad, wanting to move out of Tulsa, where her son's father had recently married another woman. Both Rachel and Erin had liked her immediately and had hired her on the spot.

Marissa had rented a small apartment outside of town and would be commuting every day until her lease expired and she could find a place in Desire. Rachel had at first thought of Kelly's old apartment above Indulgences before remembering that Frank Elliott lived there now.

Marissa's main concern, however, was her son and what she would do with him while she worked. It occurred to Rachel that she'd soon be in the same position. She talked to Boone and Chase about it one night over dinner.

"How am I going to take care of the baby while I'm working?" she asked them.

"Baby," Boone leaned forward and touched her arm. "You do know that you don't have to work. Chase and I can easily support a family."

"You want me to give up my store?"

"No, baby. If you want to work there, fine, but you don't have to."

She sat back in her chair and sighed. "What am I going to do?"

Chase plopped a spoonful of mashed potatoes onto her plate. "You have that room in the back that you're not using. Why don't you let us fix it up as a little nursery? That way Marissa can keep her son with her, and you can keep the baby with you. We'll ask the Prestons to build some furniture for it, a crib and maybe a little table and chairs. Boone and I can build something to store toys in."

Chase grinned at her surprised look. "What? Didn't you think I could come up with a solution to your problem?"

"No. I mean, yes. I don't know why I didn't think of it before. That would be wonderful!" She chewed at her lip. "But I'd really hate to leave them alone while we're busy out front."

"Ask Amy and Lily to babysit," Boone said quickly before Chase could say anything. He smiled at his brother's glare. "Edna said they're looking for jobs. Amy graduated at the end of last year so she could probably work during the day.

Rachel jumped up and threw herself into Boone's arms. "You are a genius."

"Hey," Chase protested. "I had the idea about the nursery."

Rachel smiled and walked over to him. She placed a hand over the zipper on his jeans. "After dinner, I'll show you just how much I *appreciate* the work you're going to do on it."

Chase's cock jumped to attention beneath her hand, and her breath caught at his wicked grin.

"Well, all right then." He nodded and pulled her onto his lap, moving his hand under her shirt and over her stomach. "Your jeans are unfastened."

"I can't button them anymore," she told them both ruefully. "I'm going to have to shop for maternity clothes soon."

"We'll drive into Tulsa whenever you want." Chase's smile grew as he continued to rub her stomach. "He's going to need some room."

"Rachel," Boone leaned forward, his expression sober. "We have to go get a license and make the arrangements to get married."

"I've already told you," Rachel began and tried to stand, but Chase kept her on his lap.

"Our baby is not going to be born a bastard!" Boone thundered. "You think about that. You're going to marry us as soon as possible. I'm not playing this game anymore. That's it!" He stormed from the room, more angry than Rachel had ever seen him.

She heard the front door slam, followed by the slam of the door of his truck. He started the engine and roared out of the driveway.

Rachel felt her eyes well with tears and looked up at Chase sadly. "I don't know what to do," she whispered brokenly.

"Yes, you do. Don't cry," he said gently, wiping her tears away with his thumbs. "Go take your bath while I clean this up. Boone will cool down and be back in a little while."

"I'll help you."

"Go. Relax in the tub. I'll be there in a few minutes." He tilted her face to his. "You know that we love you, don't you? It has nothing to do with the baby. You getting pregnant just made us realize that our fears almost made us miss something that we both want very much. We're not letting you go, Rachel. No matter what."

Rachel got to her feet, her heart heavy. Glancing out the window she thought of Boone's anger. How could she know for sure? But did she have the right to deny her baby his fathers? Then again, what would it be like for a child to be raised in a house where his fathers married his mother out of a sense of obligation?

She had a lot to think about and she felt too tired to deal with it tonight. She'd assumed she'd have the time to decide what to do but Erin, Boone and Chase all kept trying to pressure her to get married right away. She thought about it as she relaxed in her bath, warm and lethargic.

Why not? They'd been getting along just fine and she felt happier than she'd ever been. They seemed happy, too. Of course they were very excited about the baby but she didn't miss the way they looked at her, how they constantly touched her. Boone always pulled her onto his lap and rubbed her feet. Chase always rubbed her stomach and played with her hair.

She would do it. She would marry them. The baby needed his fathers and at least she knew they cared for her.

Stepping from the tub, she dried off, humming to herself as she thought about Chase's reaction. Seeing Boone's reaction would have to wait until he got home from his temper tantrum. Hanging up the towel, she frowned when she saw the red on it, momentarily dumbfounded. Panic set in when she looked down and saw a streak of blood on her thighs.

"Chase!" Rachel screamed, afraid to move. A sob broke free as fear froze her in place.

"Rachel?" She heard him race down the hallway and into the bedroom. Seconds later he appeared in the bathroom doorway. Seeing her horrified expression, he froze. "What is it, honey?" he asked softly as he approached her.

"I'm bleeding," she told him in a terrified whisper.

"Oh God, honey." He looked down. "Don't move."

He raced out of the room and came back with a blanket, bundled her into it and lifted her gently into his arms. He laid her on the bed, clutching her hand in his as he called the doctor. When he hung up, he turned tortured eyes to her. "He'll meet us at the hospital. He said he might need the equipment there."

A minute later he lifted her gently into his truck and raced for the hospital.

* * * *

Chase had never been so scared in his life. He drove to the hospital like a madman but carefully kept his voice tender as he spoke to Rachel. She gripped his hand like a lifeline with both of hers, and he brought them to his lips often as she sat next to him shaking.

He knew that her horrified expression as she showed him the blood on her thighs would haunt him for a long time.

"Everything's going to be fine, honey." He prayed that he spoke the truth. The way she looked up at him so trustingly made him feel so helpless. She depended on him to be strong for her and make everything all right while inside he quaked in fear and knew it was out of his hands.

"Should we call Boone?"

Yes! He wanted to shout. He wanted his brother here badly, but didn't want to let go of Rachel's hand long enough to call him.

"I'll call him from the hospital. Don't worry, sweetheart. Just try to relax." He smiled at her and he hoped it reassured her. "Don't you worry. That baby's staying right where Boone and I put him, nice and cozy inside his mama."

God, he prayed for enough strength to keep her calm long enough to get her to the hospital before he completely fell apart. The trip seemed to take forever, and he kept talking to her the entire time, not even remembering what he said. Finally the hospital came into view and Chase squealed the truck to a stop at the emergency room entrance. Lifting his precious burden from the seat, he raced inside.

Doc Hansen stood just inside waiting for them. "Bring her back here. I've got a room ready for her."

Chase followed him, carrying Rachel to a room in the back, tightening his hold as she trembled even harder in his arms. "I'm right here, honey. Try to calm down. Take a deep breath for me."

He laid her gently on the bed as a smiling nurse came into the room and started to unwrap Rachel from the blanket. "Let's get you unwrapped so the doctor can take a look at you."

Rachel gripped his hand again and looked up at him. The love and fear in her eyes nearly undid him. "Chase, I'm scared."

He leaned over her, caging her in, his mouth inches from hers. "I know, honey. Me, too. But Dr. Hansen is here. No matter what, we'll get through this together. I promise."

Rachel reached up to touch his face. "Call Boone. I think we both need him."

As they prepared Rachel for her exam, Chase pulled out his cell phone.

"You can't use that in here," the nurse told him. "You'll have to step outside."

He glared at her. "I'm not leaving Rachel."

"Go." He looked down to see Rachel looking up at him, her eyes filled with tears. "Go call Boone. We both need him here. But come right back."

Knowing that she was right and that Boone did need to know what had happened and get his ass here, he leaned down to kiss her forehead. Even there he felt her trembles. "I'll be right back, honey."

He cursed as it took him three tries to punch in his brother's number.

"Boone."

"Boone, we're at the hospital," Chase managed to choke out. His heart pounded, and he paced nervously as he gripped the phone tightly.

"What? Oh God! Is Rachel hurt? Is it the baby? What happened?"

When Chase spoke again, his voice broke. "Rachel's bleeding. She's with the doctor now. I have to get back to her." He took a shuddering breath. "Boone, she's really scared. I'm scared. Get your ass here fast. We both need you here."

"Okay. Try to calm down and keep Rachel calm. I'm on my way. I'm sorry I wasn't there. You two just hang on. I'll be there as fast as I can. I'll pick up Erin. Rachel's gonna want her there."

Chase had already started back inside as he disconnected.

* * * *

"I was so scared." Rachel rubbed her face into Chase's hand as he leaned over her. "Thank you for being so strong for me. I know you were scared, too." She had seen the fear in his eyes as he'd kept her hand gripped tightly in his during her exam.

The nurse had wanted him to leave but Dr. Hansen had told her that Rachel would be better off if Chase stayed, especially when he realized what had happened.

The bleeding had already stopped by the time they'd arrived and the doctor assured them that junior was fine and right where he belonged.

"It's such a relief." Rachel felt tears wet her cheeks again. "Now that it's over I can't stop crying." She sobbed. Chase's arms closed around her, pressing her against his chest. She buried her face in his throat as he murmured softly to her.

"Oh God. No."

She heard Boone's tortured moan and lifted her face, turning to see Boone and Erin standing in the doorway. He strode to the other side of the bed, leaned down and reached for her, pulling her tightly against his chest.

"It's okay, baby. We'll make more babies together, I promise. I'm so sorry. I love you so much, baby." Rachel clung to him, stunned when his voice broke.

"She's okay," she heard Chase tell them. "The baby's okay. Rachel's fine. Her blood pressure spiked and caused the bleeding."

Boone stiffened and lifted his head. "They're okay? They're both okay?"

Boone gripped her face between his hands and lowered his face to hers. She saw tears glistening in his eyes before he moved in to kiss her tenderly. "You scared me, baby." He dropped another kiss on her lips before moving as Erin nudged him aside.

"Everything's really okay?" Erin asked, worry tightening her features. "Both you and the baby are alright?"

"Yes," Rachel smiled and leaned against Erin, wrapping an arm around her. She closed her eyes when she felt her sister's hands in her hair, hugging her close.

"Thank you, God!"

Erin released her and Rachel looked up in time to see Boone pull Chase from the chair and embrace him. After relieved smiles and back slapping, Boone grabbed Chase by the arms. "I'm sorry I wasn't there. It won't happen again." He looked over at Rachel. "I'm sorry, baby."

Rachel nodded and smiled through her tears. "Poor Chase probably needs a drink about now." She reached for Chase's hand. "He was so good and held my hand the whole time."

She lay back down and Chase pulled the blanket over her. "After this maybe I won't be such a wreck in the delivery room."

"What did the doctor say?" Erin demanded of Chase.

"They want to keep her overnight for observation."

Boone's smile disappeared. "Why? What's wrong?" He moved to Rachel and gripped her hand again.

Chase sighed and stood, leading Erin to the chair. "He says her blood pressure is a little high. He wants to monitor it overnight and make sure there's no more spotting. If everything's okay, she can go home in the morning. But she has to go into Doc Hansen's every week to monitor her blood pressure."

Rachel listened with half an ear, drowsy now after all the excitement. When Boone released her hand, she moved it to cover her stomach, comforted by the slight swell there. Thank God her baby was okay.

"You said the doctor thinks her blood pressure spike caused the bleeding?"

When Chase nodded, Boone rubbed a hand over his face. "It's because I yelled at her. We could have lost the baby because of my temper."

That woke Rachel up. "No. Don't think like that. It wasn't your fault at all. It was mine."

Boone frowned at her. "What are you talking about? None of this is your fault."

Rachel felt tears prick her eyes again. "It is." She lowered her gaze, picking at a thread on the blanket. "When I was taking my bath I was thinking that if it wasn't for the baby, I would know if you really loved me or not."

"Stop it, both of you." Rachel looked up to see Erin with her hands on her hips looking at both of them. "The baby's fine and you two are blaming yourselves for something that didn't happen." She looked at Rachel. "You calm down. No more crying. No more excitement for you."

That made Rachel smile. She relaxed against the pillow. "No excitement at all?" She looked at Boone and Chase. "Where are you two going to live?"

Chapter 8

It had been three weeks since the night at the hospital. Three weeks since Boone and Chase had made love to her.

Rachel wondered if it was possible to die of sexual frustration.

The doctor had assured them that it would be perfectly safe to resume sex. On her weekly visits to Dr. Hansen, he had pronounced her fit, her blood pressure normal. Since Boone and Chase had gone with her, they knew it and still hadn't had sex with her.

That didn't mean they didn't shower her with attention. They'd gone shopping with her and Erin for maternity clothes, carrying her packages and waiting patiently while she tried things on. Afterward they'd taken the women to eat and, much to Rachel's embarrassment, Boone had lifted her feet to his lap in the restaurant, afraid that her feet may begin to swell.

She wanted to burn their pregnancy books.

They bought a sofa for the nursery so she would have a place to lie down. At least one of them brought lunch for her every day, eating with her and making sure she ate enough. She could only imagine what the next six months would be like.

Although they gave her their attention all the time, touched her frequently, there had been no sexual advances from them. She'd begun to worry that they no longer found her sexually attractive. Her belly had swelled only slightly, not noticeable under her clothes, but it did show when she removed them.

Both men loved touching her stomach and talking to it but that's as intimate as it got.

She woke each morning to two hard cocks pressed against her, but since she no longer suffered from nausea, they gave her a quick kiss on the forehead and scrambled from the bed without using them.

She wanted to scream.

Finally she decided to take matters into her own hands. She woke one morning to hear noises from the kitchen and the shower running. Smiling at the feeling of déjà vu, this time she headed for the shower. Carefully easing the bathroom door open, she saw Chase through the shower door, turned slightly away from her.

She grinned when she saw that he had also decided to take matters into his own hands. Already wet, the sight of Chase jerking off had her growing even wetter. She shucked her sexy nightie—which hadn't worked at all—, reached for the shower door and stepped inside, feeling him stiffen as she rubbed her breasts against his back and reached her hand around him.

"Rachel, damn it! What are you doing?"

She gripped his hard length, amazed as always that she couldn't circle it with her hand, and began to stroke him. "If you have to ask, I guess I'm not doing it right," she purred into his back. She bit him as she kept moving her hand. "Let me take care of this for you."

He jerked from her grasp and spun around, grabbing both of her wrists in one large hand and pressing them over her head against the shower wall. He looked down her body as she did his, and his cock jumped before he squeezed his eyes closed.

She tried to rub her nipples against his chest but couldn't move close enough to do it. She wanted him so badly, she shook. "Move closer and let me wrap my legs around you," she moaned. When he didn't, she began to struggle to get free. "Fuck me, damn it!"

Chase kept his eyes squeezed shut. His breathing sounded ragged and his cock looked so hard and more than ready, but still he wouldn't touch her anywhere but her wrists. "No, Rachel. I'm. Not. Fucking. You."

That fact that he spoke to her through clenched teeth did little to appease her. Not when she felt this aroused. It pissed her off that she couldn't make him take her. He appeared to be holding onto his control by a thread, but he still held on. She needed him to want her so much that it snapped.

She couldn't keep the hurt from her voice. "You don't want me?"

His eyes popped open, and he looked at her incredulously. "Are you out of your fucking mind? Do I look like I don't want you?"

"Then why?"

"What the hell's going on in there?" Boone opened the shower door, scowling at his brother.

"Get her the hell out of here," Chase said to him, and she found her hands transferred to Boone's as he pulled her out of the shower. "She snuck in here while I was taking a shower."

"You weren't taking a shower. You were jerking off."

Rachel spun to Boone. "If you two don't want me anymore just say so."

Boone pulled her from the bathroom with barely concealed fury. He laid her gently on the bed but Rachel knew that if she hadn't been pregnant, he would have tossed her. He quickly straddled her, lifting her hands over her head and pressing them to the mattress. He looked down at her damp nakedness, and her pussy flooded at the heat in his eyes.

"We're not making love to you again until you marry us. We've asked but we haven't pressured you because we don't want to upset you. We don't want your blood pressure to go up again. Once you marry us, we'll fuck you all you want."

Rachel narrowed her eyes at him even as a thrill went through her. They still wanted her and wanted to marry her. Reality set in. They still found it easy to do without sex with her.

The stinkers wanted to control her with her need for them. She needed them to need her so much that they lost control. They wanted her to give in first. Well she couldn't let them get away with that, now could she? She couldn't marry them while they thought they could use her needs for them against her while they had no trouble resisting her.

Oh no. She couldn't let them get away with that. She had to make them give in. Then she would marry them. After they fucked her, after they needed her as much as she needed them. She smiled up at Boone. "We'll just have to see who gives in first."

Boone smiled back at her and flicked a tongue over a nipple, making her arch and cry out. Bastard. She narrowed her eyes at him again when he smiled at her smugly.

"Let us know when you're ready to give in and marry us."

Rachel forced herself to answer coolly while an inferno raged inside of her. "I'll let you know." Right after you give in and fuck me, she thought to herself, satisfied when his own eyes narrowed and he got up to shower.

* * * *

The next day she smiled as she worked on a display, thinking about the incident this morning.

Chase had forgotten his wallet and had come back into the bedroom as she'd begun to dress for work. She had just reached into her lingerie drawer as he strode into the room.

"I thought you'd already gone," she told him, hiding a smile at the look on his face as he took in her nudity.

"I, uh, yeah," he murmured, never taking his eyes from her body.

Deciding to give him a show, Rachel bypassed the cotton bras and panties she usually wore for work and pulled out a pastel pink teddy. She donned it slowly, watching Chase out of the corner of her eye as he stared at her.

The thong teddy had been cut very high on the sides, molding her body like a second skin, even the slight belly. The cups that held her breasts high had been made of lace and her nipples could be seen clearly through them. With her long hair, she looked naked from the back.

"Damn it, Chase. What's—" Boone's words trailed off as he walked into the bedroom.

She picked up her earrings, purposely dropping one and bent at the waist to retrieve it. When she heard low groans from behind, she stood and faced them squarely, knowing that they could see everything through the sheer lace.

"Is something wrong?"

They both had bulges in their jeans, their faces tense, their eyes filled with lust. It was several long seconds before Boone spoke.

"That's not gonna work, you know." He folded his arms over his chest and smiled at her mockingly. "No matter what you do, we're not fucking that hot little body until you marry us."

"We'll see," she countered with a wink and turned to get dressed. When she turned back again, they had gone.

She giggled. This had become all-out war.

Having a lingerie shop gave Rachel a huge advantage, one she would use against them without remorse. She knew she would marry them. They'd proven that they cared for her, but she couldn't marry them until the need was no longer one-sided. They'd resisted her for almost two years. She had to show them that they wouldn't be able to do that ever again.

They would definitely give in first.

* * * *

Rachel had definitely underestimated her men.

They, along with their bulging muscles, tight asses and sneaky minds arrived at her store in time for lunch. They'd finished her organizers and ordered supplies for Blade and Kelly's house and had been hard at work on the room in the back.

Erin was off today, so she and Marissa had been about to get sandwiches when Boone and Chase walked through the door with bags in their hands.

"Marissa, we brought sandwiches for you and Lily, and Gracie fixed something for Sammy." Chase smiled at the young woman and handed her a container. "Gracie cut up a hot dog for him and put in some mashed potatoes and apple sauce."

Marissa blushed and thanked them, taking the bag into the back room, leaving Rachel alone in her small kitchen with her two big men.

She couldn't help but notice how the muscles in their arms and chests shifted as they reached for a napkin. She watched their throats work as they took long drinks of their iced tea. When Chase reached past her to start collecting their trash together, his arm brushed a nipple, and she caught her breath as they immediately hardened, plainly visible through her shirt. She eyed him suspiciously. He appeared to ignore her but she could have sworn she saw his lips twitch.

All afternoon they tormented her. They came out into the store to ask her opinion on things all day, *accidentally* brushing against her, leaning over her, their breath on her neck and generally making her crazy.

She did notice, with no small amount of satisfaction, that they had become just as aroused as she had. If she had to go through the day with a soaked teddy between her legs at least she knew they had the discomfort of trying to work with their large cocks pushing demandingly against their zippers.

Deciding that she had to beat them at their own game, Rachel went into the other room to make a phone call. When she'd finished, she struggled to hide her grin until closing time.

When Marissa and Sammy, along with Lily, finally left for the day, Rachel struggled to contain her excitement. After balancing the day's receipts, she straightened the kitchen, listening to the loud noises coming from the back.

Walking into the back room, she blinked in surprise at what had already been done. "We'll finish up the rest of this on Sunday," Boone told her when he saw her. "I don't want to paint while Sammy or you are in here. With Rafe, Sloane and Brett helping, we can do everything in one day."

They'd cleaned everything out of the room and when Marissa left even pulled off the molding and ripped up the carpet.

"Wow," Rachel said, looking around. "And all of this can be done in one day?"

"Sure, sugar." Chase put an arm around her shoulders. "Boone and I will have you ready in no time."

Rachel narrowed her eyes. "What did you say?"

"The room will be ready, sugar." Chase leered at her. "What did you think I said?"

"Uh, huh," she replied suspiciously.

Deciding to go for the kill, she shook off Chase's arm and started to walk away. "I have to go. I have an appointment at the spa." Knowing they followed her, she went out to the counter and bent to get her purse. "You guys go ahead and eat. I'll have a salad at the spa. Can you guys lock up? I don't want to be late."

"What time are you going to be home?" Boone demanded.

Rachel pursed her lips. "I'm not sure. I'm getting my hair trimmed and my nails done, like I usually do, but I've never had the rest done before and forgot to ask how long it takes."

Boone followed her to the door. "What 'rest', Rachel? What are you having done?"

With both of them now looking at her suspiciously, she could no longer hide her grin. "Oh, didn't I tell you? I'm having my pussy waxed."

She closed the door on their startled expressions.

* * * *

Several hours later, Rachel returned home to find the house well lit but empty. Puzzled, she looked around and found a note on the kitchen table. *Poker game at club. Call us when you get home.*

"Damn, damn, damn."

Prepped, aroused and feeling naughty with her men nowhere around. She'd ended up having a full treatment, and she'd been exfoliated, had been made soft, smooth, fragrant, waxed and rarin' to go, and the house was empty.

She smiled when she realized they knew they'd be unable to resist her tonight so they avoided temptation by going to the club. Strolling into the bedroom, she dropped her purse and began pacing at the foot of the bed, chewing on a recently manicured thumbnail. If only she could get to them.

She couldn't get into the club. Blade, Royce and King had always been very strict about that, and nobody could get past them or their butler/bouncer Sebastian.

But she knew her men wouldn't come home for a while. They'd want to make sure she fell asleep first. If only she could find a way to get in. A sudden thought occurred to her. Oh, yeah. That just might work.

She raced for her phone, pausing to take a deep breath before dialing. She had to call the men to tell them she'd gotten home, but insidiously to find out if they were still at the club. Three phone calls later, Rachel raced back into the bedroom to change her clothes.

She stepped into a pair of crotchless black panties, smiling at her reflection. Grinning wickedly, she put on a black bra that had holes cut into it so that her nipples poked out. She threw on a short black sundress and little black flats and raced out the door.

"I can't believe we're really going to get inside the club." Erin practically bounced on the passenger seat in excitement. "If you had done this without me, I would have hurt you."

Rachel laughed. "I know. That's one of the reasons that I called you. Also," she admitted, "I'm scared to death. The only women allowed inside are the subs that come in. I hear they go down to the club and have sex with the single men."

"What if we walk in on Boone and Chase fucking one of them?" Erin asked outraged.

Rachel shook her head. "They wouldn't consider themselves single." She waved a hand. "Jesse and Nat explain it better, but since they're with me, they won't do that anymore."

She looked over at Erin. "It's like this. In the club, only the single men are allowed to touch a woman. Single in Desire means that the men aren't married and haven't claimed a woman. Boone and Chase have claimed me. I live with them and I'm pregnant with their child. They're no longer considered single in the club and the other members would not like it if they acted as if they were."

"Oh." Erin considered that for a moment. "Do you ever wonder how many times they have?"

"I really don't want to know," Rachel muttered as they pulled into the parking lot.

Kelly had instructed Rachel about what door to go to, and Rachel found it easily. Kelly answered right away so she must have been waiting close.

"Come in," Kelly gushed, smiling over her shoulder at an approaching Sebastian. Kelly quickly made the introductions and led the women to a sitting room, Sebastian following close behind.

"Would you ladies care for some wine? Or some milk?" he asked, smiling at Rachel.

"Oh, Sebastian, that would be wonderful," Kelly gushed at him. "You're such a sweetie."

Sebastian smiled indulgently at Kelly, obviously fond of his employer's wife.

"How nice of you to visit," Kelly said to them for Sebastian's benefit.

The women made small talk as Sebastian served the wine and the milk, waiting impatiently for him to leave the room. When he finally did and closed the door behind him, Kelly jumped up.

"Come on. We have to hurry," she told the women and ran to another door. "Sebastian will tell Blade, Royce and King that the two of you are here and they'll immediately go tell Boone and Chase."

Rachel watched Kelly open the door and look out into the hallway, checking both ways before turning back to them. Putting a finger over her lips, she whispered, "Follow me."

"Wait!" Rachel grabbed Kelly's arm. "I don't want you to get into any trouble with Blade."

"Are you kidding?" Kelly laughed softly. "My husband is way too sure of himself. We're becoming so *married*. I've got to keep him on his toes."

Erin paused. "You won't get into trouble, will you?"

"Oh yeah," Kelly giggled. "Come on."

* * * *

Chase placed his bet and looked over at his brother "How long do we have to wait before we can go home?"

Boone glanced at his watch. "At least two hours. She should be asleep by then." He looked across the table at Clay and Rio. "Thanks for meeting us here."

Rio laughed. "No problem. We know how it is, believe me. It wasn't that long ago that Clay and I had problems and wanted somebody to talk to. These women are something. We have to all stick together."

"Yeah, well, you guys are lucky." Chase sighed. "Your woman married you, and she loves both of you like crazy."

"And we love her," Clay nodded. "But it wasn't easy to get Jesse to agree to marry us."

"But Jesse's more easygoing, not stubborn like Rachel," Chase muttered.

Clay and Rio froze, incredulous looks on their faces. "You're kidding, right?" Rio asked.

Boone looked at them both and chuckled. "That bad, huh? Well at least she loves you."

"Rachel loves you two idiots, too," Clay told them, placing his bet. "Although why she put up with waiting so long for you, I have no idea. If it hadn't been for the fact that everyone knew she wanted you two, she would have been taken off the market months ago."

Rio sorted the cards in his hand and nodded toward the two men on the other side of the room. "Law and Zach would have been happy if she had cared about them the way she cares about you two."

Chase scowled and turned to where the two men had a gorgeous redhead between them. They each had a hand on a breast and Law's other hand covered her mound while his brother stroked her ass. The woman had her head thrown back in ecstasy as the brothers worked in unison to drive her wild. Chase didn't like the thought that it could have been Rachel between them and his temper flared. "They can find another woman," Chase growled. "Rachel's belongs to us."

"You just have to convince Rachel of that. She sounds like she isn't sure that you love her." Clay sighed. "It's a fine line. You have to show them that you love them and would do anything to make them happy, but at the same time, you can't let them walk all over you."

"Let them know they not only have all your love, but also your protection, even when they don't think they need it," Jared Preston said, speaking softly as he looked at his cards.

"Jesus," Reese Preston complained. "You guys are turning into pussies." He pointed at Boone and Chase. "These two can't even go home until their woman falls asleep."

Reese brows went up at the look on Jared's face. "What?"

"When we finally find a woman that we can share a life with, I can see that you're going to be spending a lot of nights on the sofa." Jared's eyes were icy as he stared at his brother. "If we're ever lucky enough to find what they have, she's going to have to be a strong woman to deal with the three of us. You don't try to break a woman like that. Sometimes you have to give in."

"Even if she tries to kick me out of my own bed? I don't think so. No woman is going to lead me around by the nose."

Clay looked up at Reese. "I think you'll learn quickly that once you claim a woman, the bed is hers and it's up to her if you share it or not."

Reese stood and slammed back his whiskey. "Damned women."

Duncan Preston muttered something under his breath and got up to refill his drink.

"What's wrong with Duncan?" Chase asked, turning in his chair to watch his friend.

Jared and Reese exchanged a look. Finally Jared gestured toward Clay and Rio. "Ever since Jesse came to town and you guys claimed her, a lot of men, like us, started to feel that time is running out. I'm Clay's age, and Duncan is the same age as Rio. We don't even have any kids and sometimes it feels like we're not going to."

Clay clapped a hand on Jared's shoulder. "We felt exactly the same way right before Jesse came along." He looked at Duncan when he returned. "Just when we had just about given up on finding her, there she was."

"Gentlemen."

Everyone looked up at Blade's approach.

"Another married man," Duncan muttered.

Blade smiled, his teeth white against his dark skin. "Yes, and I don't seem to have the trouble with my woman that these guys do. I guess she knows who's boss." He looked over at Boone and Chase. "Do you know that Rachel and Erin are both here?"

Boone leapt to his feet. "What?"

"They're visiting Kelly."

"I don't like this," Chase muttered. "She's up to something. She's trying to get to us because we didn't give in earlier."

"She's trying to show you that she won't be ignored," Blade told them with a smile. "For your own sake, just make sure she gives in first. A woman has to respect her man's position."

Boone sat down again heavily. "Shit." He looked at the others. "She went to the spa today."

"Christ, man. You're done for," Rio muttered.

Chase looked at Boone. "What are we going to do now?"

"Hi, guys. Blade, this is a really nice place."

Chase turned when he heard Rachel's soft voice, knowing the others did the same. Women didn't come here. Not women like Rachel and Erin, anyway.

"Rachel!" Chase shouted in surprise.

"What are you doing here, Rach?" Boone asked softly. Chase heard the anger and disbelief in his brother's voice.

"Blade, this is really nice. Can we get a drink?" Erin smiled mischievously at the cold look on Blade's face.

"Ladies, I believe you know that you're not allowed in here." He moved to stand between them and the activity across the room.

The other men apparently realized just what had happened and that women from the town had come into the room, and they all jumped from their chairs to block Rachel and Erin's view of Law and Rem with the redhead.

Chase grabbed Rachel and slapped a hand over her eyes but Erin strained to watch the show.

"Hey, Rach, is that how it is with two men?"

Duncan happened to be the closest to Erin and grabbed her from behind and covered her eyes with his hands.

"Hey!" she protested, but Chase saw he kept her from moving.

"Would you ladies care to tell me just *how* you got in?" Blade asked in a dangerously soft voice.

"The door was unlocked, darling." The men spun to see Kelly approaching; craning her neck to see who made the noise across the room.

Blade cursed under his breath as he reached out to grab his own errant wife, whipping out a blindfold from his pocket and tying it on her.

Clay laughed. "Trust Blade to have a blindfold in his pocket." He lowered his voice. "I guess Boone and Chase aren't the only ones who are having a problem teaching their women who's the boss."

Blade ran a finger down his wife's cheek, looking dark and menacing. "We'll just have to see about that, won't we, love?"

Kelly's cheeks flushed, and Chase smiled when he saw how much Blade looked forward to taking care of his wife.

Duncan leaned down to whisper against Erin's ear. Whatever he said to her caused her to shiver.

Chase turned to a scowling Boone. "Let's get them both out of here."

Chapter 9

The men hurriedly escorted a giggling Rachel and Erin outside, both struggling to get free as soon as they got to the parking lot. To Rachel's surprise, Jared and Reese strolled closely behind.

"Let go of me." Rachel still laughed as she tried unsuccessfully to pull her arm out of Boone's grasp.

"Be still, you little hellcat. If you weren't pregnant I would have thrown you over my shoulder. Besides, your dress is so damned short, everyone would have seen your ass."

"Well maybe some other man wants to see it. You two certainly don't."

Boone grabbed her by the upper arms and pulled her to her toes. "I'm going to see it tonight, baby," he growled dangerously, his eyes gleaming with lust. "As soon as we get home, I'm going to turn it bright red." He looked over at Erin, who continued to struggle against Duncan's hold. "As for you—"

"May I speak to you a minute?" Jared came forward and exchanged a look with Boone.

Boone and Chase stared at Jared for several long seconds, and Rachel tried to interpret the look that passed between them.

Reese and Duncan stared at Erin in a way that reminded Rachel of hungry wolves. What the hell was going on?

"This is my future sister-in-law," Boone said. "If you're playing some kind of game—"

"I've never been more serious," Jared told him somberly.

Boone walked several feet away with Jared and Reese, leaving Rachel and Erin with Duncan and Chase.

Rachel smiled at the men. "You can let go of us now, you know. We're not going anywhere."

"You know you're in big trouble, don't you?" Chase rumbled in her ear before releasing her.

"Yeah, yeah, yeah." Rachel waved a hand and looked at Duncan. "Are you going to let go of my sister?"

Duncan looked at her then back at Erin, studying her sister for several long moments. Rachel didn't think he wanted to let go of Erin at all. *Mmm, something's up there.*

Finally Duncan released Erin, running a hand down her arm before stepping back. He shared a look with Chase, but Rachel couldn't interpret the look that passed between them so she turned to her sister. Putting her arm through Erin's, she moved several feet away.

Erin's hands twisted together nervously. She'd also turned bright red. She kept shooting glances at Jared and Reese, then hurriedly looking away. When her gaze slid to Duncan, Rachel could feel her tremble.

"Do you know them?" What the hell had happened? Erin didn't ruffle easily.

"Of course not. Where would I have met them?"

"Calm down, Erin, Jeez, what's with you? Desire's a small town. You could have met them anywhere." She sobered at the look of panic on Erin's face. "What is it, Erin?"

Erin's face cleared. "Nothing, sweetie. What could be wrong? Look, the men are coming back. Give me your car keys so I can drive home."

"Jared will be driving you home," Boone told Erin as he approached, Jared and Reese right behind him.

"But that's not—"

"Something you want to argue about," Boone finished for her. "You're already in enough trouble."

"Trouble? I'm a grown woman."

"Do you remember our talk?" Boone asked.

Erin went still beside her. Her whispered, 'yes', sounded shaky.

"Do you live in Desire?"

Erin lifted her chin and glared at Boone. "I could leave."

Uh oh. Something about this seemed terribly wrong.

"Erin, what's the big deal about Jared driving you home?" Rachel looked up at Jared who smiled at her reassuringly before turning back to Erin.

Erin hugged her. "Nothing. Go on home with your men. I'll be fine."

Rachel couldn't help looking at Jared again, surprised when he came forward and dropped a kiss on her forehead. "Don't worry, sweetheart. Your sister is perfectly safe with me."

She felt Boone's hand on her bottom, as he leaned down to whisper in her ear. "You'd be better off worrying about yourself, baby. You're in a lot of trouble."

Rachel felt the heat from his hand on her bottom. Combined with the rumble in her ear and his breath on her neck, she could already feel her body preparing for pleasure. She had gone years without sex before, but now that she'd experienced the pleasure they could give her, she couldn't go long without making love with them. It had been weeks! She had to make them give in soon or she would go crazy.

She laughed softly and patted his arm, trying hard not to show her excitement. Saying goodbye to everyone, she turned and walked toward Boone's truck as if she didn't have a care in the world. Inside she bubbled with delight and need.

* * * *

Rachel walked into the house and strode straight to the kitchen, intensely aware that Boone and Chase followed close behind.

"Don't try to avoid your punishment, brat." Chase moved to lean against the counter.

Rachel reached past him for a glass and moved to the refrigerator for the orange juice. She glanced over at Boone, who stood leaning against the doorway. She poured her juice, leaned back against the counter and watched them while she sipped it.

"Why did you come to the club, baby?" Boone asked softly.

"I thought I'd just drop in to say hi."

Boone smiled. "You're lying."

"Why were you trying to avoid me?" she countered.

Boone sobered. "We weren't trying to avoid you. We went to play poker."

"Now who's lying?"

Boone straightened and started toward her. "You know you have to be punished for going in there."

Rachel smiled and sipped her juice. "No, I don't believe I do."

"Excuse me?" Boone's lips twitched, and Rachel wanted to laugh.

She shrugged. "I was lonely. I just wanted to see my men. I shouldn't be punished because I missed you, should I?" She finished her juice. "It's been a long night. I'm going to bed."

She brushed past Boone and strode into the bedroom, hiding a smile when she heard their footsteps behind her. If they wanted to make her pay for her actions tonight, she had a debt to collect from them as well.

Walking into their bedroom, she kicked off her shoes and, appearing to ignore the men as they undressed, went to put them away. Meeting their stares, she reached for the hem of her dress. She pulled it over her head and tossed it aside.

The matching looks of stunned stupefaction on their faces as they stared at her bra almost had her laughing out loud. She walked to the mirror on her dresser to remove her earrings but ostensibly to watch them from the corner of her eye.

Having already removed their shirts, they stood staring at her wearing only their jeans. She turned to face them, smiling coyly. "Do you like what you see?"

"Very much," Boone said softly but with a wicked smile.

Chase moved close and reached out to touch a nipple. Her eyes fluttered closed at the exquisite jolt.

"I've never seen a bra like this one before," Chase's mouth teased as his hands did. "You're so soft, honey, and you smell so good," he said against her nipple before taking it into his mouth.

They turned her, and Boone moved in behind her. When a muscular thigh pressed between hers from behind, she eagerly spread her legs wide. Chase's mouth moved from one nipple to the other, his hands hot at her waist. Boone's hand slipped between her thighs, and she leaned back against him. His lips nibbling at her neck froze. He spun her around and dropped to his knees in front of her, ignoring his brother's 'Hey'.

"Well, well, well," Boone drawled, and Chase knelt down to join him.

"Do you like my panties?" she teased.

"What there is of them," Chase replied, touching her folds, plainly visible.

"Enough of this," Boone growled harshly and reached for her panties.

"No." Rachel reached out to stop him. "Stop ripping all my bras and panties. Let me take them off."

"Hurry up then," Boone said through clenched teeth.

Rachel reached behind her to unclasp her bra, taking her time and watching their hungry looks as they remained on their knees in front of her.

"Rachel," Chase growled in warning. "The hell with this." He grabbed her panties, stripping them down her legs.

Rachel laughed at their impatience and cocked a hip forward. "So what do you think of my wax job?"

"Jesus." Boone breathed and ran his fingers over her bare folds.

"Damn, sugar." Chase looked up at her, the gold in his eyes more pronounced. "You are the most beautiful thing I ever saw."

"I was home all alone," Rachel pouted. "I got all waxed and smoothed, and the men who say they love me went out to play poker." She covered her breasts with her hands. "My breasts are soft and smooth and there wasn't anybody home to feel them."

Chase grinned. "Oh, honey, I'd love to feel how soft and smooth your breasts are." His hands closed over them. "Damn, they are soft."

Boone pushed one of his brother's hands out of the way to take one of her breasts in his own hand. "Hell, they're even softer than before."

Rachel felt powerful and desired as her two hulking lovers knelt before her, apparently enthralled by her breasts. When they gently pinched her nipples, she moaned and fell forward, bracing a hand on each of their shoulders. She cried out when she felt a hot mouth on each nipple and tangled her hands in their hair to hold them to her.

Boone raised his head. "I want that bare pussy." His mouth moved over her stomach, working its way lower. "Oh, baby. You're in trouble tonight." Then he put his mouth on her.

With Chase's hands and mouth on her breasts and Boone's on her slit, Rachel's knees went weak. They both knew her body well and every touch had been designed for maximum effect. Boone's hands on her hips held her firmly in place to create the magic in her that he was oh so good at. She hadn't been prepared for just how sensitive her bare folds would be.

When Chase moved a hand to her bottom, she unconsciously clenched it in anticipation. They touched her everywhere, keeping her right on the edge.

She heard her own breathless groans and tortured mews as though from a distance. Her whole body quivered in lustful anticipation, but they wouldn't give her the last little bit she needed to come apart.

Chase's hand continued to play with her bottom, his finger teasing her puckered opening fleetingly, then moving away to caress her buttocks. His hand on her breast cupped its weight, sliding his palm lightly over her nipple, but not giving her the friction she needed. His mouth on her other breast kissed and nipped, occasionally licking a hard nipple with the flat of his tongue, but not giving her the satisfaction of closing his mouth over it.

Boone used his tongue masterfully, stroking every bit of her so fleetingly that she felt it all over but it didn't stay long enough for her to process it before he moved again. He pushed his tongue inside her, stroking her just long enough for her to anticipate the next thrust before moving away. He licked her folds, working his way toward her clit, but as soon as her body tensed, frozen in expectancy for the next touch of his tongue that would send her over, he poked into her again.

A sharp nip from each of them here and there kept startling her back from the brink, and within minutes, she had become so fiercely aroused that all she cared about became reaching for pleasure. She didn't understand their murmured comments to each other over her own cries or the roaring in her ears. She didn't know that they'd lifted her to place her on the bed until she felt the cool crisp sheets at her back. She whimpered in distress when their hands and mouths left her until they gently flipped her to her stomach.

Rachel felt something against her cheek and opened her eyes to see a throbbing cock directly in front of her, the head looking angry and red. She dove on it, taking it into her throat in one fell swoop, starving for the taste of her men. She sucked frantically as if her life depended on it, and she heard a tortured hiss followed by cursing and harsh gravelly moans as she feasted. She dug her hands into Chase's hips, her nails digging into his muscular butt and, catching him off guard, yanked him down on the bed. She pulled his legs under her arms before he could stop her.

She attacked him with a vengeance, using her tongue on him and sucking hard, vowing to take away every shred of his control completely. Something inside her had to prove to her lovers that she could make them mindless with passion every bit as much as they made her. Still miffed about the way they'd tried to avoid her earlier, she had to show them she wouldn't be ignored.

Chase's cursing got more violent by the second as he tried to pull away from her in desperation. That just made her more determined.

Boone slipped a finger inside her dripping pussy, and she immediately began to move on it. She could only imagine the sight she made, pumping her bottom at him as she fucked herself on his thick finger. Hoping he wouldn't be able to resist much longer, she kept moving, which kept Chase's cock moving in and out of her mouth.

Now she heard Boone's curses as she wiggled her ass at him. His finger slid out only to be replaced with a thick cock. He slid to the hilt inside her as strong hands on her hips tried to still her movements. She fought them and kept thrusting herself onto Boone's cock over and over and felt a sharp slap on her bottom.

"Damn it, Rachel."

She ignored them and kept moving, not giving either man a chance to recover. She needed to show them that not only could she handle both of them at the same time, but she could drive them both crazy with desire until they no longer had any defense against her.

"She's clamping down on my cock like a fucking vise!" Boone slapped her ass again. "Ease up, baby. I want *you* to come."

Rachel gloried in her lovers' responses and doubled her efforts.

"Damn it, Rach." Chase's voice sounded breathless and tortured, and the muscles in his thighs trembled under her hands. Rachel knew he was close. Very close.

She used her inner muscles to clench and release on Boone's cock, fighting her own impending orgasm with everything she had.

"Ohhh, fuuuuck!" Chase screamed hoarsely as he came, spurting his seed down her throat, shaking as she continued her smooth strokes, only easing up when he had been licked clean.

"Ease up, damn it." She thrilled at Boone's tortured groan, and the slapping on her bottom continued as he tried to get her to relinquish her tight grip on his cock.

Chase finally managed to extricate himself from under her and quickly moved down the length of her body.

The heat from Boone's slaps had heated her pussy even more, and it had become a fierce battle to see which one of them could last the longest.

"Let go, damn you!" Boone's tortured yell sounded like music to her ears, heard over her own frantic cries and moans as she struggled to hold off her orgasm. Boone's hands tightened on her hips, forcefully trying to control her thrusts while Chase reached one hand under her and placed a rough finger over her clit, her own movements providing the friction.

Seconds later a thick finger pressed into her bottom and she knew she'd lost. She gripped it hard as she gripped Boone even harder and she couldn't hold off any longer. An incredible orgasm began to wash over her.

Huge swollen waves of it rolled her over and over. Boone plunged deep, holding himself still as he pulsed out his own completion, his primal roar making her heart sing. It soothed her ego, slightly dented, that they could stay away so easily, even as it thrilled her that they knew it had been necessary in order to resist her.

The usual ease in which they usually had her coming over and over had been blissfully absent as she finally succeeded in taking them to the brink of their own control and pushing them over. It had taken both of them scrambling frantically to see to her pleasure before she forced theirs on them.

But she had sent Chase over first, she remembered in delight.

She lay collapsed on the bed, her men on either side of her. They all breathed heavily, trying to recover, and Rachel couldn't wipe the grin off her face. They used their hands and lips on her as they usually did after sex as she touched both of them. She had a hand on each of their chests, her lips against Chase's shoulder. She loved the connection, the feeling that they still wanted to touch her even afterward.

"You look like the cat that swallowed the canary," Chase chuckled tiredly.

"It wasn't a canary and it seemed to like being swallowed very much," she drawled.

"God knows," he agreed. "Jesus, Rachel, if you ever do that again—"

"You'll react the same way." She smiled, exhausted.

Boone chuckled. "Well at least one of us was able to hang on long enough."

"Barely." Rachel giggled and turned her head to face him, smiling drowsily.

"Yeah," Chase agreed. "And you needed my help or you would have been a goner. It's a good thing I was able to get my hands on her, or you wouldn't have made it."

Boone lifted his head and looked over Rachel to stare at him, lifting a brow. "That's because she'd already made you come. The second she latched onto you, you were done."

"Wait until she does that to you."

Chase lifted up on his elbow and ran his hand up and down Rachel's back, enjoying the feel of her soft skin. "Honey, Boone and I weren't really trying to avoid you. We were just trying to stay away from temptation until you agreed to marry us." When there was no response, Chase continued, afraid that Rachel may still be angry. "We love you, honey, and it's time to stop these games."

Boone, lying on the other side of her, dropped an arm over his eyes and sighed. "That's right, baby. We wanted to have your promise to marry us before we made love to you again." Boone chuckled. "I guess you won that one, but now you have to marry us."

When there was still no answer, Chase looked at his brother. Boone lifted his arm and opened his eyes. Turning to face Rachel, Boone chuckled. "She's sleeping."

Boone lifted her while Chase moved the tangled covers and they settled her between them.

"Damn, I love her," Chase breathed, dropping a kiss on Rachel's shoulder and tucking the covers around her.

"So do I. And I want her married to us as soon as possible. I have no idea how we stayed away from her as long as we did."

"Yeah, I know what you mean." He chuckled, almost asleep. "Christ, when she attacked me like a little she-cat my control was shot. I never stood a chance."

Boone looked down at Rachel as she shifted and sighed, then adjusted the blanket over her shoulder again. "We're going to have to make sure that the next time we make *her* lose it."

Chase settled back and closed his eyes, grinning. "Yeah, we definitely have some planning to do." He cuddled closer to their future bride's back, heard her sigh contentedly in her sleep and knew he'd never been so happy in his life.

Chapter 10

The next morning Rachel woke disconcerted to find herself alone in bed. She sometimes did when they had an early job, but she could hear voices coming from the kitchen. Normally, they'd have stayed in bed to cuddle or make love to her as soon as she woke up. She hated this feeling of insecurity that kept rearing its ugly head. She needed to feel desired for herself and not that they only wanted her for the baby. This insecurity really pissed her off.

After showering and slathering on her moisturizer, she combed the tangles out of her curls and left her hair loose to air dry. Donning only a robe, she walked to the kitchen, following the tantalizing aroma of coffee and the equally tantalizing low rumbles of her men. She found them both there, Boone sitting at the table and Chase leaning against the counter. Both wore their usual faded jeans, t-shirts and worn work boots. She wanted to eat them up.

"Good morning." She smiled at them both hesitantly and moved toward the coffee.

As she went past Boone, he snagged her wrist and pulled her onto his lap. A large rough hand slid under her robe to cover a breast, her nipple beading against his palm as his mouth covered hers. He tasted of coffee and mint and she couldn't help but pull his head down, her hand tangling in his thick hair, trying to get closer.

He chuckled against her lips as she squirmed against him before taking her mouth hungrily. He deepened the kiss, rubbing his palm over her breast, rasping her nipple and creating a delicious friction.

Already her pussy wept in need, and when Boone lifted his head, she tried to pull him back down. He removed the hand from her breast, sweeping the robe aside and looked down her body, completely exposed to his gaze. She arched her breasts upward and his eyes glittered with desire. It warmed her clear through when they looked at her this way, and it pushed all her insecurities aside.

"You are so beautiful, baby," he murmured softly, running a hand over her body. "You take my breath away."

"Look at you," Chase breathed and knelt on the other side of her and leaned in to take her mouth with his.

Her slit dripped as Chase took her mouth teasingly. Both men ran their hands over her, completely avoiding her where she needed it most.

"Oh God," she moaned as she felt their rough hands on her.

"I didn't get to eat that soft pussy last night," Chase crooned. "It's definitely mine this morning."

Lying back with Boone's strong thighs supporting her, Rachel felt Chase move lower, shouldering his way between her thighs. He gripped her bottom in his hands and lifted her to his mouth.

Boone held her as she squirmed on his lap, his strong hands providing the security she needed to forget about everything except Chase's mouth on her slit.

His mouth moved all over, his tongue poking at her puckered opening and moving back to her folds, licking them thoroughly before using his tongue to press inside her dripping pussy, then closing on her clit.

Then he started all over again.

She cried out her pleasure as she gripped Boone's arms, imagining the picture she presented to him, splayed out on his lap, her skin flushed, while his brother drove her wild with his mouth.

Rachel jolted when a hot hand closed over a nipple and rubbed it lightly just as Chase sucked her clit sharply. His teeth scraped the throbbing nub gently and she went over.

Screaming her pleasure, her toes curled. Her whole body tensed as it washed over her, shards of pleasure racing through her.

They brought her down gently, their soft strokes allowing her to float back to earth. She felt herself being transferred to Chase's arms as he moved to another chair and sat with her cuddled on his lap. Her head fell to his shoulder, her hand over his chest as he settled her on his thighs.

"Good morning, honey," he chuckled, dropping a kiss on her hair.

Rachel giggled but didn't open her eyes. "Good morning. I just came out for some coffee." She started to reach for the button on his jeans.

"And instead you got some sugar." Chase laughed and rubbed her hip before, pulling her hand away. "No time for that this morning. We have to go get the permits for Blade and Kelly's new house."

Rachel sat up as Boone placed a cup of coffee on the table in front of her. "Why are you two still here?"

"We wanted to drive you to work today," Boone told her and sipped his coffee. "We want to take you to the hotel for dinner tonight. We'll stop by and pick you up as soon as the store closes. Okay?"

Rachel smiled and hoped it didn't look forced. "Sounds good. I'll take a dress to work so I can change there." She got up and took her coffee with her to the bedroom to get dressed, her smile falling as soon as she left the room.

Why hadn't they made love to her? She'd certainly been aroused enough. They'd given her pleasure but when it was over that had been the end of it. Although she'd reached for Chase, he'd quickly pulled her hand away. She walked into the huge closet, wondering what in the hell she was going to do.

* * * *

Chase watched Rachel walk out of the room and stood. "My dick is so hard I could pound nails with it."

Boone adjusted his own jeans. "Tell me about it. I came close while she was wiggling on my lap like that. But we can't keep fucking her like animals. She's pregnant for God's sake. We have to see to her pleasure, and when we take her, it has to be nice and slow so we don't hurt her or the baby."

"She certainly should get pleasure out of what we have planned for her tonight." Chase could hardly wait. He and Boone were dying to take her to one of the privacy booths at the restaurant. They just had to pick up a few things first.

They both sipped their coffee in silence for several minutes.

Chase finally turned to his brother. "Do you really think she'll marry us now?"

Boone sighed. "God, I hope so. I want to take care of both her and the baby."

* * * *

Rachel paused in the hallway when she heard Chase's voice. "Do you really think she'll marry us now?" She heard Boone's reply. So that's all it was. They wanted to take care of her. She definitely had some thinking to do. Pasting a smile on her face, she walked into the kitchen. "I'm ready."

* * * *

The dress Rachel had chosen to wear to dinner was plain black, the neck square cut. It had been cut a little fuller at the bottom with a flirty skirt that came about mid thigh. Her straighter cut dresses had been a little tight around the middle and tonight she wanted to look her best.

Her stomach fluttered in anticipation and fear. Either it would work or it wouldn't but she would soon know one way or the other.

When she saw her men get out of the truck, she was glad that she'd dressed up. They both looked gorgeous in their dress clothes, each wearing black dress pants and a button down shirt. Boone wore a white one, Chase wore black.

Rachel's nerves got worse as they pulled into the parking lot of the hotel restaurant and she began to tremble. If this didn't work, she didn't know what she would do.

When they entered the restaurant, Brandon stood waiting for them. He greeted the men and turned to Rachel. "I've already congratulated your men but I haven't had the chance to congratulate you yet. You're a beautiful mommy to be." He raised her hand to his lips and said under his breath. "Everything is ready. I hope you know what you're doing."

She answered just as quietly. "I have to know."

"Get your own woman," Boone growled and pulled Rachel against him.

Brandon looked at Rachel pointedly and laughed. "They seem to be crazy about you. Come this way, and I'll show you to your table."

Following Brandon across the dining room and through a heavy curtain, they came to a candlelit booth away from the other diners. "Oh, how beautiful!" Rachel smiled at the men. "This is very nice."

"These booths are reserved for special occasions," Chase told her proudly as he helped her into the booth.

She didn't say that she'd seen it earlier this afternoon but there hadn't been candlelight then. Brandon turned to leave, and Rachel jumped up. "I'm sorry, but could you show me where the ladies room is?"

Boone smiled. "I'll take you."

"No! I mean no, that's okay. I'm starving. Please get some bread or something that I can nibble on. Junior's hungry." She followed Brandon back through the curtain before they could respond. He led her to a table where Jesse sat with Clay and Rio.

All three stood when they approached. Jesse came straight to her. "Are you okay, honey?"

Rachel laughed shakily. "Yeah, just nervous." She looked up at Jesse's husbands. "Thank you for doing this for me. I know how you men all stick together."

Clay leaned down and kissed her forehead. "We're still on Boone and Chase's side. This is what you need and whether you believe it or not, your needs come first with them. Are you ready?"

Rachel dropped her hand over her fluttering stomach and nodded. "Yeah. I hope so."

Rachel sat with Jesse while Clay and Rio entered the privacy booth where Boone and Chase waited. She heard muffled voices but couldn't tell what had been said. She winced when she heard Boone's curses and a few minutes later Clay and Rio strolled out, both wearing huge smiles.

"Your men are ready for you." Rio chuckled as he helped her from her chair. "But I wouldn't keep them waiting."

When she reached up, he bent down so she could kiss his cheek. "Thank you so much. Are they mad?"

"I think they're upset and confused. You need to get in there." Rio smiled at her encouragingly. "Go take care of your men."

Rachel nodded and walked to the booth where she could still hear curses. She paused to take a deep breath before entering. Walking inside, she was torn between laughter and crying when she saw Boone and Chase struggling against their bonds.

The booths had rings attached in strategic places and her men were cuffed hand and foot to the rings.

"Rachel, you'd better explain this." Boone struggled against the bonds while Chase just stared at her.

"You don't really want me. You only want the baby."

When Boone opened his mouth to protest, Rachel held up a hand to silence him. "I heard you this morning. You didn't want me even when I was naked on your lap. I heard you say that you want to take care of me and the baby."

Boone's brows went up. "But we do want to take care of you and the baby. That doesn't mean we don't want you. If you heard everything we said, you would know that we almost came in our jeans this morning."

"If that's true, then why didn't you make love to me?"

Boone sighed. "You're pregnant, baby. We don't want to hurt you."

"Well you did. I don't want you to treat me like I'm made of glass. I'm a woman, and I want to be made love to by my men. If you won't do it, then I don't want you around."

"We'll just see about that. Undo these fucking cuffs."

"No. If you want me, I should be able to tell before the night's over."

"What do you mean by that?" Chase growled.

"You'll see." Rachel pushed the button on the table and a waiter came in carrying an assortment of foods. They set it up to her earlier specifications and pulled the table several feet from the bench Boone and Chase sat on and quickly left.

"Now before we begin, let's make the two of you more comfortable. And remember, if you make a lot of noise the other people in the dining room can hear you."

Chase yelled. "I don't give a fuck if they hear me or not!"

Rachel smiled. "You wouldn't want them running in here to see if everything's alright, would you?"

"I don't care."

"Mmm. Well maybe you'll care now." Rachel whipped the dress over her head and laid it across the bench. Standing in only a garter belt and stockings, she did a slow spin. "Now would it be okay for someone to come in?"

Sliding her hands up her body, she cupped her breasts, lifting them deliberately. Both men stopped struggling to watch her, their eyes widening. "What are you doing, baby?" Boone asked. "Get these cuffs off, and let Chase and I make love to you."

She leaned back against the table and deliberately dropped the key for the cuffs onto it. She smiled at a still struggling Boone and started toward him. He stilled again when she straddled his thighs and leaned in, touching her lips to his. When he tried to deepen the kiss she pulled back and waited, shaking her head at him. He sat back, his eyes narrowing. Still she waited, raising a brow at him. When he finally nodded, she started to move in slowly once again. This time he stayed still and allowed her to trace his lips with her tongue, and she felt the shudder go through him. This was fun.

Leaning back, she reached for the first button on his shirt and undid it, moving her way down the rest of them and kissing and running her tongue over every inch of his muscular chest as it appeared. She touched his hot skin, gently stroking, loving how his big body trembled under her hands. His erection pressed against her, and when he lifted up, she moved away.

"Come on, baby. Undo the cuffs and I'll take you right here," Boone growled. She smiled when she noticed that he'd kept his voice low.

 She turned to him and placed a finger over her lips. "Shhhh." She moved to the table and picked up a piece of shrimp and traced his lips with it. His teeth closed over the shrimp, his eyes never leaving hers. "Good boy." She patted his cheek and moved to Chase.

Straddling him, she leaned forward and smiled against his lips when he didn't move or speak. Tracing his lips with hers, she darted her tongue inside. When he tried to tangle his with hers, she moved away, pleased when he moved to follow her. Waiting until he settled back, she did it again, and this time he opened his mouth and allowed her to do what she wanted.

She used her tongue to trace all around his mouth, loving the way his body trembled like his brother's. Leaning back, she unbuttoned his shirt, one button at a time, kissing and licking his chest as she did. She sucked one of his nipples, loving the way he gasped. She leaned back and shook her head before straightening and moved to the table to pick up another shrimp. He obediently ate it, and she could see his struggle to remain still.

Moving back to Boone, she positioned herself between his legs and licked one of his nipples. He tightened, and she looked up to see that he bit his lips to keep from making the same mistake as his brother. She rewarded him by sucking the other into her mouth, loving the shudders that wracked his body.

Leaning back, she reached for his belt, undid it and his pants, and he lifted obediently so she could pull them and his boxers to his knees. His cock was hard and pointed straight at his stomach. She looked up to see that his hands had tightened into fists above the cuffs.

She got up and moved to the table and got a stuffed mushroom and put it against his lips, grazing her nails over his sack as she fed him.

Moving to Chase, she hid a grin as he arched upwards at her approach, and she undid his trousers in the same way. She fed him a mushroom and wanted to laugh at the look of disappointment on his face but he didn't say a word. She traced a fingernail over the tip of his angry looking erection, and he bit his lip to keep from making a sound.

Moving back to the table, she dipped her finger into the cocktail sauce and spread it slowly over her nipples. She glanced up occasionally to see their eyes riveted on what she did and saw their cocks jump in reaction. She licked the rest of the sauce off her finger, humming in appreciation and reached for a shrimp.

"I'm sorry that I didn't offer you cocktail sauce before for your shrimp. Would you like some?"

Boone opened his mouth to speak, apparently thought better of it, and nodded.

"Good boy."

She put the shrimp to his mouth, and he bit into it hungrily and stared at her nipple expectantly. She moved closer, placing her nipple at his lips, and he closed his mouth on her, licking all the sauce away.

Rachel felt the jolt all the way to her pussy which had already become wet and needy. Reluctantly, she pulled away and looked over to see Chase licking his lips expectantly. She plucked another shrimp from the tray and watched his cock jump again as she got near.

"Would you like some sauce with your shrimp, too?"

He nodded immediately, and he bit into the shrimp. When she offered a sauce covered nipple, he latched onto it hungrily. Her pussy clenched in need, and she bit her lip to keep from crying out. He sucked her nipple hard as though afraid she would pull away from him. This is what she needed. She wanted them so hungry for her that they only thought about how much they needed her.

Chase's cock jumped against her stomach, and he groaned deep in his throat. She looked over to see Boone watching what they did hungrily, his eyes dark. His cock looked ready to burst.

She pulled away from Chase and smiled. "Are you getting hungry for me?"

He smiled at her evilly, and her slit flooded as she turned and went back to the table. Picking up the small bowl of cocktail sauce, she moved toward Boone. "I wonder why they call this cocktail sauce. Should it be eaten from a cock?"

She watched, fascinated as his sack drew up and his cock jolted. Reaching in with her finger, she scooped up some of the sauce and moved to spread it on the head of his cock. His cock jumped at her touch so she had to hold it still to finish.

His breathing grew harsh, and he groaned deeply in his throat as she spread the sauce around the plum sized head. She turned to walk slowly back to the table, looking over her shoulder to see that he watched her ass the whole time. She picked up a shrimp and walked back toward him, kneeling between his legs and watching as he closed his eyes and took a deep breath before opening them again.

She bit into the shrimp and leaned forward, using the flat of her tongue to lick the sauce from him.

His thighs trembled under her hands, and she loved the feeling that washed over her. She felt more desired than ever as if they would do anything she wanted to get a taste of her, a touch from her.

He groaned constantly now as she licked him, and she looked over to see Chase watching intently, his own cock jumping.

"It *is* better with the sauce, isn't it?"

She picked up the bowl again and moved toward Chase, again having to hold his cock still as she smeared the sauce all over the head. He swallowed heavily as she bit into the shrimp and arched his hips forward. She licked him clean as he twisted on the bench, groaning when she moved away.

Moving back to the table, she sat on the edge and spread her legs wide. Both men stared at her bare folds and she used her fingers to part them. A thrill went through her when they both began to struggle against their bonds again.

"I don't like having men who won't fuck me. I have needs, too. Sometimes I like to be fucked really hard by the men I love." Her pussy had become soaked and she knew they could see her juices as she opened herself to them. "I'm starting to think that you don't want to fuck my pussy hard anymore." She got off of the table and walked toward Chase, moving close and separated her folds to his gaze.

"Do you think it's fair that I have a wet pussy and no one to fuck me?"

"No. Undo these cuffs and I'll fuck your pussy, honey."

"Hard?"

"Oh, yeah." He struggled against the bonds again. "Undo these fucking cuffs and I'll fuck you so hard you'll beg for mercy."

"Promise?"

"Yes, undo the fucking cuffs now!"

She turned to see Boone watching her and straining against his own bonds. Walking toward him, she swayed. God, she loved the way his eyes devoured her. "My poor bottom need to be fucked really hard." She turned her back to him and bent, rubbing her puckered opening against his cock.

He automatically surged forward, and she giggled. "Do you want to fuck my ass really hard?"

"When I get out of these cuffs, I'm going to shove my cock so far up your ass that you'll feel it in your throat. Get these fucking cuffs off. Now!"

Rachel giggled and walked away although it had become nearly impossible. But she knew what happened next would make it worth her while. She picked up her dress from the bench and pulled it on over her head, smiling at the look of surprise on their faces.

She plucked two large napkins from the table and placed one over each of their straining cocks. "Don't knock those off or you'll be really embarrassed when you're rescued."

"Where the fuck do you think you're going?" Boone roared.

"If you want me you'll have to come and get me," Rachel smiled over her shoulder and walked through the curtain.

Brandon stood with a smile on his face as he handed her a key. "Room 103, sweetheart."

She reached up to kiss his cheek, smiling happily. "Thanks." She heard Boone yell for her. "Just try to give me a few minutes head start."

* * * *

Less than five minutes later, Rachel sprawled naked on the bed in the hotel room. Boone and Chase came barreling through the door, coming to a halt when they saw her.

"Do you have any idea how hard it is to zip your pants when your dick is hard enough to break concrete?" Boone growled at her.

"If you both come here I'll see what I can do to help you with that."

Both men undressed so quickly she thought she heard rips, and then they were on her. Chase dove for her pussy, shoving his way between her legs and attacking her with his mouth. Before she could draw a breath, he'd rolled her so that she was now on top of him. He ate at her as though starving and she couldn't even catch her breath as he held her thighs firmly for his mouth to ravage her.

Behind her, Boone moved in. His tongue started at the top of her crease and worked its way down. When he got to her forbidden opening, he licked and bit at her hotly, mercilessly.

She grabbed onto the headboard for support as both men held her firmly. Her orgasm approached quickly, and she shook at its force, crying out her surprise that it had hit her so fast. Their mouths never slowed, and she hadn't come down from the first before they had her racing for another.

Her voice became hoarse from her cries but that only seemed to turn them on even more. Their mouths felt hot and hungry and did such erotic things to her body that she didn't think she could survive it.

At some unspoken cue, they suddenly stopped. Chase slid up the bed as Boone helped to position her, pressing her down on Chase's cock, and she whimpered at the sudden full feel of him inside her. Chase grabbed her hips and began thrusting as Boone used her plentiful juices to lube her, fucking her ass with his finger in time to Chase's thrusts. Their hands were rough, their grunts primitive as they held her, opened her.

Feeling them at both openings and hearing their deep moans, which had become even louder, Rachel thrilled at their loss of control even as she knew in the back of her mind that they wouldn't hurt her. Boone's hand at her shoulder held her still as he told his brother to stop.

Boone worked his cock into her bottom with none of his usual finesse. He shoved inside her. The pinch and burn of it had her tightening on them both, and she came again.

She absently heard them curse and Chase's shoulders were slick with sweat as the stroking resumed. They fucked her hard, harder than they had even their first time together. The painful pleasure sent her spiraling, and she wanted it to last forever. They plunged into her over and over, grunting and groaning without their usual rhythm. She loved it!

They wanted her. They wanted her so much and had become so aroused by her that she knew only she could satisfy their hunger. She gave herself completely, letting go. They stiffened and held their pulsing cocks deep inside her as she satisfied their lust. The loud sounds they made and the feel of both of them pulsing deep inside her shot her over once again.

She collapsed on top of Chase, moaning as Boone slowly slid from her to collapse beside them. The only sounds in the room were groans and heavy breathing for several long minutes.

"Jesus, baby. Did we hurt you?" Boone pushed her hair back from her face and studied her intently, his eyes full of concern.

"Oh God." Chase moved Rachel to lie between them, rubbing a hand over her belly.

She reached up to cup one of their cheeks in each of her hands. "The only way you could hurt me would be to make me feel like you didn't want me the way I want you."

Both men rubbed her belly as they kissed her lingeringly. Boone chuckled. "Well I think you can be sure never to feel hurt again. Damn, I thought I was going to come in your mouth when you licked that sauce off of me."

"Jesus." Chase rolled to his back. "I don't think I've been out of control like that since I turned nineteen."

"Good." Rachel sighed tiredly. "I wouldn't want to marry someone who didn't want me."

Both men rolled to look at her. Boone touched her cheek. "I hope we showed you just how much we *do* want you, baby."

Rachel smiled contentedly. "You did, and thank you."

"Thank you!" Chase laughed. "I'll never again be able to eat shrimp cocktail without getting hard."

"We never did get to eat dinner," Boone said. He snuggled closer.

She didn't care about dinner. She heard their deep breathing as Boone and Chase started to drift off. Smiling, she snuggled between them. Apparently her men didn't need dinner either. She'd already satisfied their hunger. With that thought she drifted off to sleep, smiling as she went under.

Epilogue

Both Boone and Chase had shown her how much they desired her even as their lovemaking had gentled. Telling her they'd never forgive themselves for hurting either her or the baby, they'd slowed their lovemaking but it was no less thorough.

Rachel bubbled with anticipation as she got ready for bed. Today, their wedding day, her men had promised her a surprise tonight and had eyed her wickedly all day. She couldn't wait to see what they had planned for her.

Nude, she walked into their bedroom to find them both waiting for her. She glanced at the bed, surprised to see three jewelry boxes there. Eyeing the boxes curiously, she saw they were all from Jake's jewelry store.

"You look beautiful, baby. I love you so damned much." Boone moved toward her and leaned down for a kiss. He lifted his head, his eyes glittering and moved behind her. She felt his heat at her back a second before she felt his hands reach around to cup her breasts as Chase moved in for his own kiss.

When Chase lifted his head, he smiled wickedly and handed her one of the boxes. "I love my new bride, too."

Rachel smiled at each of them before opening it. They watched her expectantly. Inside she saw a gold chain with loops on the end.

What in the world? Her brain had turned to mush as Boone continued to play with her nipples. She picked it up and looked at it closely. "What is it?"

Chase grinned. "Allow me."

Rachel watched, stunned, as Boone cupped her breasts while Chase looped one of the rings over a beaded nipple, turning a small screw she hadn't seen to tighten it in place.

"Oh, it feels, it feels—"

Boone's voice rumbled in her ear as Chase attached the other. "Does it feel good, baby?"

"Oh yes."

Chase removed his hands to look at his handiwork as Boone looked down over her shoulder.

"Very sexy," Boone murmured and touched the chain to make it swing.

Rachel reached back to grip his shoulders, gasping at the erotic pull.

"Maybe a little tighter," Boone told his brother. Chase grinned and moved to tighten them even more.

The sensation was more than pleasure, less than pain, and Rachel gripped Boone tighter, moaning deep in her throat. "Oh God, it feels so good!"

Boone chuckled against her neck. "Well, we have to buy our wife pretty things, don't we?"

Chase picked up another box from the bed, turning it toward her before opening it.

She'd never seen anything like it before and had absolutely no idea what it was. It had been made of gold, the top shaped like a teardrop with three small chains hanging from it. Each chain had a tiny ring at the end.

Rachel looked up at Chase in confusion. "It's beautiful, but I have no idea what it is."

Chase grinned wickedly and removed it from the box, throwing the box on the bed with the others and holding the object in front of her. "See this little loop at the top?"

Rachel nodded and eyed him suspiciously, groaning when Boone sent the chain attached to her nipples swinging again.

"It goes around your clit."

Rachel's hands tightened on Boone even more and she gasped. "You can't be serious."

Chase's grin grew. "See, I put this in my mouth and suck your clit through it. Then I use this little screw to tighten it so it won't come off."

"Oh God!"

"It keeps the hood back so your clit stays completely exposed. It also keeps your clit swollen and very, very sensitive."

"I won't be able to stand it."

Boone nipped her shoulder and sent the chain swinging again, drawing another moan from her. "See how the chain moving pulls at your nipples? When you move, the chains on that will also do the same thing to your clit."

"Oh no."

"Oh yes." Chase laughed and knelt at her feet as Boone pushed a hard thigh between her legs to spread them.

Chase moved quickly, sucking her clit sharply through the loop, moving back and tightening it before she could come.

It felt incredible! Her clit had never felt so sensitive. She could even feel the air move on it as Chase moved. With another devious grin, he sent the three chains dandling from it swinging. Rachel cried out, gulping air desperately. Her clit felt huge and the chains pulled devastatingly as they moved.

"Oh my God." Sharp little sparks spread from her clit and raced throughout her body. Recognizing the early warning signs, she expected to go over.

But the sensation just continued.

Boone came around her and they both stared at the jewelry they'd given her. Boone looked at her face and smiled. "We can't take you roughly for a while but there are things we can do to show you just how much we love and desire you. You're just going to have to get used to our way of showing you." He paused as she groaned. His tone hardened. "Walk to me."

Rachel's knees went weak at that tone. When he continued to stare at her, she hesitantly moved forward and her knees nearly buckled at the motion of the chains on her nipples and her clit.

Boone wrapped his arms around her as soon as she reached him, pulling her tightly against his chest. The sensation on her too sensitive nipples made her moan.

"I'm going to fuck you nice and slow. Do you know what it's going to do to you with your clit exposed like that?"

Rachel shuddered and couldn't catch her breath. Her hands fisted on his shirt. Her legs trembled so badly it had become hard to remain standing.

Boone turned and picked the last box up off of the bed and Rachel's eyes widened. What else?

Boone grinned at her expression. "Now you really didn't think we would allow our new bride to get away with what you did to us that night at the restaurant, did you?"

Rachel looked back and forth between her new husbands and gulped. What on earth had she set free when she'd told them of her need to feel desired? She'd already gotten more than she'd bargained for and apparently they weren't through with her.

The tingles of pleasure that kept racing through her made it hard to concentrate.

Boone opened the box, and she saw a large variety of little chains, each with something dangling at the end. She saw gold beads and crystal ones, hearts, flowers and a lot of others, all in different sizes.

"These are for us to use with the jewelry we've already given you." Boone smiled and pulled a heart shaped charm out of the box, holding it in his fingers as he hooked it to the chain attached to her nipples.

"What are they?" she whispered shakily, closing her eyes briefly at the delicious pull on her nipples. He waited until she opened her eyes and looked down at his hands before letting go.

"Weights." She barely heard him as the overwhelming pleasure sent her over the edge.

THE END

www.SirenPublishing.com/LeahBrooke

ABOUT THE AUTHOR

Leah Brooke has always loved to read and has always been addicted to happily ever after stories.

After years of writing stories for her own amusement, she finally decided to submit a manuscript.

Now she writes every day and hopes her readers get the same enjoyment from her books as she's gotten from so many books over the years.

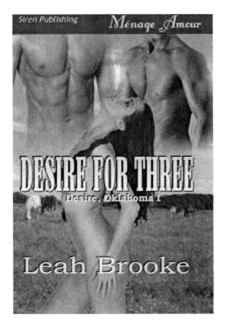

[Ménage Amour 15: Erotic Contemporary Ménage à Trois Romance, M/F/M, with Dom/sub BDSM]

With her fortieth birthday approaching and a bad marriage behind her, Jessica Tyler wants a fresh start. Marriage left her an emotionless shell and she vows never to get involved with a man again.

Giving in to her sister, Jesse agrees to visit her in Desire, Oklahoma.

But Desire is a small town unlike any other. Dom/sub and ménage relationships are the norm in a town where ranchers and cowboys adore and protect their women in ways that leave Jesse fascinated. She's first intrigued, then alarmed when two gorgeous over-protective brothers, Clay and Rio Erickson, rush to claim her for their own.

Yanked from her protective shell, threatened by her ex, Jesse is determined to stay strong, even as her two formidable lovers are intent on possessing her.

Will her independence be smothered or will love give her the strength to change all three of their lives forever?

ADULT EXCERPT 1

She had never had such feelings with any man. Not even her husband had made her feel this way before they got married. Something warmed inside her and she started to feel hope that she wasn't doomed to remain this cold unfeeling creature that she had become.

Looking up at Clay, she felt her nipples harden. He kept glancing at her as he drove, the heat in his gaze unmistakable. She felt the moisture flow from her pussy, amazed again at how much these men affected her.

"We're glad you're coming with us, honey." Folding his much larger hand over hers where they clenched on her thighs, Clay let his fingers trail over the inside of her thigh, grazing her jeans over her pussy. "Thank you for giving us a chance to see how good we can be together." His smile told her he knew the effect his hand had on her.

Feeling the need to warn them, Jesse looked straight ahead and began, "I think there's something you should know about me before this goes any further."

"What's that, darlin'?" Rio asked.

"I'm not good at sex," she blurted before she lost her nerve. She continued to stare out the windshield, not having the courage to see the disgust she knew had to be written on their faces. "I don't want you to take it personally, I mean don't blame yourselves if I can't, er, you know." She knew her face turned bright red as she continued to stare straight ahead.

"Come?" Rio asked pleasantly.

"Yes." She nodded. "I usually don't like to be touched. It turns me off. With you, though, it seems to be different, but I'm not used to it." She glanced up at Clay. "I'm not sure what will happen if your touch gets more intimate."

She felt herself turning even redder as both men laughed.

"Oh, our touch is going to get a helluva lot more intimate," Rio warned.

"Step one," he continued, "seems to be getting you accustomed to our touch. While you're staying with us, will you agree to let us do whatever has to be done to explore your boundaries?"

"Before you answer," Clay added, "be very sure, because if you say yes, you're saying yes to us doing whatever we want to do with you, touching you everywhere. If you truly don't like something, we'll stop, but if you're creaming like you are now, we're going to keep going no matter what you say."

Rio gently turned her to face him, his fingers gentle on her chin. "It's all about your pleasure, honey. Our pleasure depends on your pleasure." She gasped when his thumb caressed her bottom lip. "So, what's it gonna be? Will you agree? Will you trust us with your body, with your pleasure?"

Inhaling deeply, she whispered "Yes," before she could change her mind. Without thinking, she touched her tongue to Rio's thumb. Startled at herself, she tried to pull back.

"Oh, no, you don't." Rio pulled her onto his lap, her back against his door. "You said yes, and teased me with that little tongue. You're all ours now, darlin'."

With that, he began to kiss her, his tongue sweeping into her mouth in a kiss like none she had ever had before. He tasted like sin as he teased and cajoled with his tongue, urging her to play with him. His fingers pulled up her top and unhooked her bra until her breasts were free for both of them to see.

"Beautiful," she vaguely heard Clay as Rio continued his devious assault. He broke the kiss to pull her top over her head and remove her bra. Running his hands over her breasts, he murmured to Clay, "Feel how smooth and soft she is."

He continued to explore a naked breast while Clay reached over for his own inspection. "Baby, your breasts feel so good, soft here," he circled her breast with his callused hand, "and harder here." He tweaked a nipple, and then pinched it lightly between his thumb and forefinger.

Jesse arched as Clay and Rio continued examining her breasts, lightly pinching and pulling on her nipples as they tried to see what she liked. "Oh, God," she whimpered. Riding along in a truck, half naked while two gorgeous men played with her breasts had to be the most mind blowing experience that she had ever had. Highly aroused, she didn't even care if anyone saw her.

Jesse felt a hand undo the snap on her jeans. Rio kissed her, his hand on her breast as she felt the zipper being lowered. Rio lifted her and she felt her jeans being pulled off. Clad now in only a pair of cotton panties, she felt vulnerable and grew hotter.

She felt a hand, she didn't know whose, and didn't care, lay over her mound. "Your pussy is really wet, sugar." She heard Clay's voice, the tension in it unmistakable. "It's so hot, maybe we better get these panties off."

The way he said "panties" caused her to cream even more. She soon became soaking wet and started to feel a little embarrassed at it. She heard a rip and felt her panties being torn from her. She thought it impossible to get any wetter. She closed her legs as she felt the air from the window on her wet folds.

"Uh, uh," she heard Clay scold. "I want those thighs wide open." Moaning into Rio's mouth, she felt Clay pull her left leg until her foot touched his headrest. Rio meanwhile lifted his mouth from hers and moved her right leg until her foot pushed against the dash board.

With her legs now splayed wide open, Clay had a good view of her pussy. His eyes darkened even further as he reached for her, running his fingers through her soaked folds, then spearing a large finger inside her.

Lying naked, spread wide, with Clay and Rio's undivided attention, she felt more desirable than she had ever felt in her life. They appeared to be mesmerized by everything about her, a balm to a wound she didn't realize was so raw.

She shook so hard with desire now that she would gladly do whatever they asked of her if only they would hurry and do something! She wanted to be fucked as she never had before.

"Please," she whimpered, past caring how wanton she sounded.

"Please, what, baby?" Clay asked deviously.

He knew just what they had done to her, damn it, and more than aware of the effect it had on her. His finger was in her pussy, for Christ sake. He knew the height of her arousal and still he continued to tease her. She moved restlessly on his finger and their wicked grins told her they enjoyed the show.

"You have got to feel how tight she is," Clay told his brother. He pulled his finger out of her and almost immediately she felt another push into her.

She heard Rio moan. "If her pussy is that tight, can you imagine how tight her ass is gonna be?"

"What!" Jesse tried to close her legs to no avail. Both men had a grip on her and she couldn't move anywhere. "I don't do that!"

"Do what, darlin'?" Rio asked. "Don't get fucked in the ass?"

"I've never been taken there," she admitted, then gasped and arched again as Clay touched her clit.

"Like that, baby?"

Her mind went blank as Rio continued to stroke her pussy, adding another finger as she heard him tell Clay that she needed to be stretched a little more. She felt the truck stop and glanced out the window to see that they had pulled up in front of a two story house.

Her eyes closed again as Clay turned in his seat, keeping her legs parted for their touch. He teased her clit mercilessly, circling it until she moved to try to make contact with his finger. He avoided her easily, making her sob in frustration.

"Have you ever had anything in your ass?" Rio asked, hoping her arousal wiped out embarrassment. "A finger, a butt plug, anything?"

"Nooooo! Please, please, please! I'm ready. You don't have to wait."

Rio looked over to see Clay looking as angry as he felt. Remembering what Jesse had told Nat about her sex life, he knew she had never been played with like this. She'd obviously never had this kind of attention, had never been aroused to this extent and they had only just started.

He watched as Clay touched his finger to her clit and gave her what she craved. She arched and came in complete abandon, beautiful as her skin flushed a rosy pink. She screamed, and then whimpered like a kitten as his brother brought her down gently. He wished he could have had his mouth on her but with no room to maneuver in this damn truck he knew that it would have to wait. He would, though, he promised himself. He couldn't wait to get his mouth on that hot pussy.

He had only intended a little petting on the way home, but their little darlin' had gone up in flames. She responded so well to every touch that it surprised him that he hadn't come in his jeans. Watching her come had been more arousing than anything he could remember. Already beautiful to him, when she came she blew him away. He wanted to get his mouth on that pussy. He loved to eat pussy, and since he and Clay had all but claimed her for their own, his desire to taste her grew even stronger.

He couldn't imagine anything better than the taste of his woman's pussy.

He wanted to shove his cock inside her so deep that she would feel it in her throat. But, as tight as she felt, he and Clay would have to be gentle with her as they stretched her to accept them. They would get Jesse so hot, she would beg them to fill her.

Rio strode into the master bedroom and noticed Clay pulling down the bedding with a flick of his wrist. He looked down at the tempting bundle in his arms, completely naked, her skin flushed a rosy hue, and grimaced as his jeans became even more uncomfortable.

Laying his precious bundle on the cool, crisp sheets, he stood and tore off his clothing, his eyes never leaving the beautiful woman on the bed. Jesse eyes widened as she watched them undress, starting to look a little nervous as she saw them naked for the first time.

Rio saw how Jesse's eyes moved back and forth as she watched him and his brother undressing. He couldn't wait to sink into her, any part of her, and he knew by the look on his brother's face, that he felt the same.

ADULT EXCERPT 2

Squeezing her thighs together, she moaned as Clay's hand smoothed over the flesh his hand had warmed. She felt his hand push between her thighs. "Open your legs, baby."

Embarrassed that he would feel how wet his spanking made her, she tried desperately to hold her thighs together. Another sharp slap on her bottom made her jump.

"Open!" Rio demanded and pushed his hand so they each pulled on her thighs, parting them.

Clay chuckled and dipped two fingers into her soaked pussy. "Somebody enjoys getting a spanking." He stroked her pussy and she let her thighs part further to give him better access.

"Oh, oh, please," she begged.

"Not yet, baby. Soon," he promised.

She heard a drawer open and felt Clay's fingers slide out of her.

"No!" she sobbed. She felt him part the cheeks of her bottom and froze in surprise. A cold wetness touched her anus and she squealed again. She felt Clay's finger push the lube into her anus.

"No!" Panicked, she tried to get up but Rio held her down with a hand on her back.

"Stay still, darlin'. We have to stretch you before we can take your ass."

"Stretch me? Take my ass?" Jesse squirmed in both fear and excitement.

Rio moved forward and pushed the hair out of her face. "We don't want to hurt you, darlin'. When we take you together, you're gonna come like never before."

He rubbed a hand down her back. "And so will we." His eyes darkened with emotion and lust. "We've waited our whole lives for you. Let us make you feel good."

Jesse nodded hesitantly. "I'm scared," she admitted tremulously, not used to any of this.

Rio grinned deviously. "I would be if I were in your shoes. You're just gonna have to trust us."

Rio moved away, back to kneel at her thighs. "I'm gonna watch while Clay opens your tight little bottom, darlin'. I wouldn't miss this for the world."

Jesse could feel her face flame as Clay opened her ass cheeks wider. "The problem with you, baby, is that you've never had a man who could handle you."

He pushed one of his large fingers past the tight ring of muscle and fully into her and she gasped. "Now, you have two of them."

Jesse felt his finger slide into her. She felt the pinch and unfamiliar fullness of her rear being invaded. He stroked slowly in and out, working the lube into her.

"Oh, God!" Jesse felt her thighs being parted and a hand, it had to be Rio's, slip between them. A rough finger circled her pussy opening and she felt him push into her.

She automatically pushed back against him, inadvertently pushing Clay's finger further into her ass. The feeling, uncomfortable and unfamiliar, quickly became forbidden pleasure, her inhibitions disappearing as she opened her thighs wider. What Clay and Rio did to her amazed her. She had never had this much attention paid to arousing her.

She felt Clay pull his finger out of her and tried to follow it. She wanted to come!

"Please, don't stop! Put it back!" She heard them both chuckle, too aroused to care.

"Let's try two fingers. Then I'm gonna put the small butt plug inside you."

"Butt plug?" Jesse asked warily.

"Rio and I did a lot of shopping for you, baby. Now, let's see how well you take two fingers."

Jesse felt Clay push more lube into her and his fingers press firmly against her tight opening.

"It burns!" Jesse panted as Clay pushed relentlessly into her anus. She never felt so vulnerable and couldn't believe that this helpless feeling made her even hotter. She would bet the two of them knew it though.

Clay held her ass cheeks open and she knew both he and Rio watched as Clay's fingers stretched her. They had completely taken over her body until she no longer felt in control of herself.

She moaned as Clay continued to press into her, stretching her. The painful pleasure felt so foreign she struggled against it, more than a little afraid of how much it affected her.

"It's too much!" She protested even as she pushed against Clay's hand, taking his fingers further into her. "Oh!"

When Rio's fingers slipped from her pussy to circle her clit, she jumped.

"Easy, baby." Clay held her firmly in place as he continued stroking her. His cock throbbed, rock hard as he worked her ass, knowing how tight and responsive she would be when he finally worked the length of his cock into her tight bottom.

Her juices wet his jeans, her arousal so great at whatever they did to her. His imagination went wild thinking about all the things he and Rio had yet to do to her.

God, she responded to their every touch. Her ex had obviously never tapped into her wild passion. Now that she had experienced it, she would crave it. He vowed that only he and Rio would satisfy her.

Their passions had been denied for years and would now be turned loose on Jesse. He looked up to see Rio watching Jesse in fascination. He must have felt Clay's eyes on him because he looked up, meeting his brother's gaze.

The hunger in Rio's eyes no doubt reflected in his own. "She's ours," Rio breathed so only Clay could hear.

Clay nodded and they both looked back at the woman over his lap, the woman they both had already fallen more than half in love with. They had tapped her passionate nature and would continue to explore it, and her, thoroughly.

Clay stroked his fingers in and out of her ass marveling at how tightly she gripped them. Her moans filled the room.

"Your ass is so tight, baby." Clay knew by the way her muscles clenched that her orgasm loomed close. He wanted his mouth on her smooth pussy when she came.

Pulling his fingers from her, he grabbed one of the anal plugs they had gotten today. Knowing that they had almost no control with Jesse, they had already brought their purchases home and readied them for tonight.

Seeing the look on Rio's face, Clay handed the plug to him. They grinned at each other when Jesse squirmed.

"Please, I want to come." Jesse panted and tried to push off Clay's thighs.

She moaned, then gasped when Rio positioned the plug against her anus.

"Easy darlin'" Rio crooned to her. "Relax those muscles so I can push this plug into your bottom."

Clay felt the shivers that went through Jesse as Rio pressed the plug into her.

"Oh, God!" Jesse's moan thrilled him as Clay watched the plug disappear into her ass. He felt her shiver and wasted no time, lifting her and laying her back on the bed, positioning her legs as they hung over the side.

Clay knelt between her thighs, lifting them.

"Now I get to lap up this pussy. Come for us, baby." Clay lowered his head and sucked her clit into his mouth.

Jesse screamed as her orgasm hit her, shaking uncontrollably. She arched and shook, her limbs jerking so hard that she inadvertently dislodged Clay's mouth.

"Uh, uh, baby." He pulled her back, firmly holding her thighs in his grip. "I'm not done yet."

Rio lay naked and aroused next to her. Clay heard him murmuring praises to her and looked up to see his brother brushing the hair from Jesse's face.

"You're beautiful, darlin'." Rio's mouth covered hers as Clay's pushed his tongue into her pussy.

"Oh, baby, you taste so good." Clay breathed and resumed lapping her juices, sliding his tongue from her pussy to her clit and back again.

"Told ya," Rio lifted his head and glanced at his brother before turning his fierce gaze back to her. "And she's all ours. I'm going to enjoy eating that pussy every day."

"I want to be inside this soft pussy when you come, baby. Turn over and take Rio into your mouth."

He flipped her effortlessly onto her stomach, pulling her to her knees and positioned her the way he wanted.

"Just imagine what it's going to feel like when we get our cocks inside that tight ass." Clay pushed on the plug and twisted it.

"Oh my God!" Jesse sobbed.

Rio lifted her until she rested on his thighs as he lay back. He stroked his length with one hand, cupping the back of her head with the other.

"Come on, darlin'. Let me feel that hot mouth on my cock. I've been thinking about my cock in that mouth of yours all day."

Clay watched his brother's face and knew when Jesse took him in her mouth. He heard Rio hiss then groan.

Clay watched his brother with their woman, his love for her growing.

"Told ya." He threw his brother's words back at him and grinned as Rio's features tightened with the strain of holding off his orgasm.

"Let's see how tight this pussy is with your ass plugged, baby." Clay positioned the head of his cock at her pussy entrance.

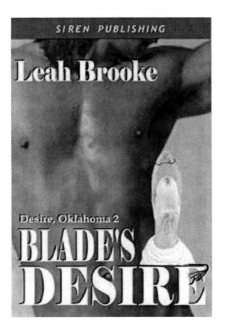

Newcomer to Desire, Oklahoma, Kelly Jones wants to get over her past. Physically and mentally abused, she wants a new start. Falling in love with a self-proclaimed Dom, Kelly wonders if she isn't in over her head.

But she underestimates Blade Royal's patience.

Little by little she falls under his spell and soon her body burns with a need she knows only he can fulfill. Her body demands relief so she makes a bargain that has her putting her trust and her body in Blade's hands for the next six weeks.

Kelly fights to hide her love from him, not knowing he's already determined to make her his own. Blade knows she has hidden passions that are a perfect match for his own.

He only has to show them to her.

She watched as Blade tapped his finger against his chin thoughtfully.

"Let me see if I understand what you want from me."

Kelly held her breath as Blade continued.

"You want me to try to fuck you, to see if you would be able to go through with it?"

Kelly swallowed nervously. Why did it sound so awful when he said it? She shook her head at her own stupidity.

"No, no, it's not like that." Keeping her head lowered, she glanced at him nervously.

"I *want* to be with you." Suddenly shy, she licked her lips. She had to make him help her. "I'm just afraid, and you've always been very patient with me."

When he said nothing, Kelly looked up at him pleadingly. "Don't you understand? I want to have sex, but I'm afraid I won't be able to let go. You're a Dom. You know how to help me do it."

At Blade's continued silence, Kelly felt her eyes fill with tears.

"Damn it, Blade. I'm tired of letting what Simon did to me ruin my life. I want to live again. I want to be able to have sex again. Please, will you help me?"

Kelly's heart skipped a beat when Blade stood and loomed over her. Kelly automatically leaned back in her chair. Her nipples tightened painfully as her stomach clenched.

Blade caged her in by bracing himself with a hand on each of the arms of her chair. His eyes held hers, making her feel as though he could see into her soul. They burned with a knowledge she didn't understand.

Nothing could have prepared her for what he said next.

"For the next six weeks, you will do whatever I tell you to do. You will wear what I tell you to wear and all of your free time belongs to me."

"I will teach you how to trust me in all things. You will have no control in what I do to you. You will do what I tell you to do without question or hesitation. If you hesitate or question me, you will be subject to punishment in any way I see fit."

Kelly felt goosebumps break out all over.

"You will trust that I know what you are capable of tolerating, concerning both pleasure and pain. You will answer every question I ask truthfully and immediately."

Kelly felt her eyes widen. She'd never heard Blade talk like this before. No wonder men came to learn from him.

What had she gotten herself into? Her body hummed, aroused beyond belief, even as she shook, thinking about what he might have in store for her.

His touch since entering the room had been completely impersonal. He seduced her only with his words. How would her body react once his touch became more intimate?

"The only way to stop whatever you feel you can't handle," he continued in that same tone, "would be for you to say the words 'red light.'"

Kelly watched as Blade straightened and moved several feet away from her, hands on his hips.

"If you say those words, it stops everything."

When Kelly frowned, Blade nodded.

"Everything, Kelly. Without trust, we have nothing. We won't be anything more than two people living in the same town. Do you accept these terms?"

Kelly felt her stomach drop. She found herself neatly cornered. If she walked away now, she would never know if she and Blade had a chance.

She loved him.

She trusted him as she hadn't ever trusted another man. Could she trust him enough to be as vulnerable as a woman could be with a man?

Kelly only knew that for the rest of her life she would regret not taking this chance.

She also had to come to terms with the fact that if she accepted, there would be no turning back.

"What happens after six weeks?" Kelly asked cautiously.

"In six weeks our agreement is over. By that time, you will understand yourself better than you ever have. In many ways. After that, we'll talk again."

At her continued silence, he raised a brow. "Do you accept my terms?"

She could do this. She *had* to do this. She had six weeks with Blade, six weeks to see if she could be the kind of lover he would need. Six weeks from now, she would have the answers she needed to get on with her life.

"Can I ask you something?" Kelly shifted uncomfortably.

"Of course, love." His eyes were gentle, though still hot.

"Will there be any other women, I mean, um, I know you train Doms and..."

"I will not be fucking anyone but you for the next six weeks. And if you think about letting anyone else touch you, you'd better think again."

Kelly took a deep breath and folded her hands on her lap.

"Then I accept your terms."

Blade kept his face blank, careful not to let his relief show. He didn't fuck the subs who came to the club, even the ones who came with their Doms who shared.

He, Royce, and King didn't fuck woman indiscriminately. They had sex, sure, but only with the women they truly wanted to have sex with.

Blade hadn't had sex with another woman since the day Jesse's ex husband attacked Kelly and Jesse. Seeing Kelly hurt had enraged him. Seeing her try to help her friend while injured had awakened something in him he hadn't known existed.

ADULT EXCERPT

Grasping her hand, he pulled her to the center of the room.

"Stay right here. I'm just going to get the cuffs. You will be restrained while I explore your body."

Oh, my God! Kelly reminded herself to breathe. She could feel the moisture on her thighs now. Why did his words excite her instead of scaring her to death?

The underlying steel in both Blade's voice and his eyes should have her screaming her safe word and running for her clothes. She feared losing control and being vulnerable. Didn't she?

She couldn't imagine doing this with anyone but Blade, though. With anyone else, she never would have made it through the door. She trusted him as she trusted no one else.

She loved him.

Hopefully, he wouldn't realize it during the next six weeks. If all went well, she would tell him after the six weeks had passed. If he found out before then, he would be angry that she had manipulated him into this. Or worse, pity her and extricate himself from their agreement.

She needed this time to be sure of herself before telling him. She needed to be sure she could be the kind of woman *he* needed.

She watched him warily as he gathered several items and returned to stand in front of her.

"You're beautiful, love."

Kelly flushed under his scrutiny.

"If that makes you blush, you're sure to be bright red long before I'm done," Blade chuckled. "Now be still while I attach these."

Kelly watched in fascination as Blade attached a cuff to each of her wrists. His eyes held hers as he lifted them above her head. Trembling, she heard a click and glanced up. He'd attached both of her wrists to a ring above her, which hung from the ceiling.

Attached to the ring, Kelly saw a thick nylon rope. As Blade pulled the rope it lifted the ring until her arms straightened over her head.

Kelly watched as he looked down at her breasts. When she followed his gaze, she flushed. Her breasts had now lifted to him as if in invitation, her nipples hard and pointed.

She closed her eyes to block the sight. She needed him to touch her breasts so badly, she ached.

"Please, Blade," she heard herself whimper.

"Please what?"

"Please touch me," she practically sobbed.

"Excuse me?"

Opening her eyes she saw Blade frowning at her. With his hands on his hips, he looked fierce and menacing and she wanted him to touch her more than she'd ever wanted anything in her life.

"I'm sorry. I can't help it. I want you to touch me so badly I can't stand it."

Blade's features softened. "I know, love. But you have to learn to wait. I'll touch you when and how I want to touch you.. *You* don't decide. I do. Now be still, so I can get your legs secured."

Blade grasped her ankles and positioned her feet a little more than shoulder distance apart, expertly attaching her cuffs to rings on the floor. Her arms now stretched even more over her head but they didn't feel pulled.

He had positioned her so that she stood completely spread and open for him.

Watching him, Kelly squirmed helplessly, desperate for his touch. She jolted when he straightened and closed his hands over her wrists.

"Are these all right? Are they pulling too tightly?"

"No." Kelly shook her head. Her heart pounded in her chest, as her breath caught in her throat.

His quick grin flashed just before his mouth covered hers. She automatically tried to put her arms around his neck and groaned when she couldn't, belatedly remembering she couldn't move them.

Her whole being felt alive in sensation, burning for whatever he would do to her. His kiss, demanding and thorough, drew from her a response she hadn't known she could give.

When he lifted his mouth from hers and straightened, she moaned helplessly.

"Now it's time to inspect my property."

Kelly knew somewhere in the back of her mind that she should object his words, but forgot everything as he ran his hands slowly up and down her arms, making her shudder and tingle all over.

She ached. Oh God, she ached. Nothing had ever prepared her for longing like this.

Blade's hands moved to her shoulders and neck, stroking lightly as he touched every square millimeter of her skin.

"You are incredibly soft, incredibly responsive. I now absolutely love the scent of vanilla."

His fingers traced under her arms and chest before moving to her breasts. With no pattern to his movements as he learned her body, she couldn't anticipate his touch in any specific place.

She wanted it anywhere. Everywhere.

He avoided her nipples and Kelly whimpered and unconsciously arched, desperate to have them touched. Her eyes fluttered closed.

When Blade lifted his hands from her, Kelly's eyes popped open and she sobbed. "Please, no! Please touch me!"

Without a word, Blade reached out and pinched her nipples between his thumbs and forefingers. Hard.

Kelly froze.

Blade's hold on her nipples tightened more and more until Kelly whimpered. "It hurts. Oh God, please Blade. It hurts!"

Blade pinched harder and she gasped, unable to struggle, stretched out this way.

"You wanted me to touch your nipples, Kelly. Isn't that what you wanted?"

"No! It hurts! Please stop."

"Are you using your safe word?"

Kelly couldn't believe the pain, but she couldn't let Blade walk away from her.

"No!"

"Are you going to let me finish my exam? Are you going to be quiet or tell me again what you think you need?"

Siren Publishing, Inc.
www.SirenPublishing.com

Printed in the United States
149068LV00004B/12/P